BBC
DOCTOR WHO

BBC CHILDREN'S BOOKS

UK I USA I Canada I Ireland I Australia
India I New Zealand I South Africa

BBC Children's Books are published by Puffin Books,
part of the Penguin Random House group of companies
whose addresses can be found at global.penguinrandomhouse.com.

puffinbooks.com

Penguin
Random House
UK

First published by Puffin Books 2015
001

Written by Justin Richards
Cover and main illustrations by David Wardle – Pickled ink
Drop capital illustrations by Adam Linley – Beehive Illustration
Copyright © BBC Worldwide Limited, 2015

BBC, DOCTOR WHO (word marks, logos and devices),
TARDIS, DALEKS, CYBERMAN and K-9 (word marks and devices) are
trademarks of the British Broadcasting Corporation and are used under licence.
BBC logo © BBC, 1996. Doctor Who logo © BBC, 2009
Cyberman image © BBC/Kit Pedler/Gerry Davis, 1966

Printed in Great Britain by Clays Ltd, St Ives plc

A CIP catalogue record for this book is available from the British Library

ISBN: 978–1–405–92655–3

BBC

DOCTOR WHO

TIME LORD
FAIRY TALES

Written by Justin Richards

Illustrated by David Wardle

PUFFIN

CONTENTS

THE GARDEN
OF STATUES

nce upon a time, there was a house at the edge of a town. It was a large house – far larger than the old couple who lived in it needed, but they had lived there since they were very young and saw no reason to leave.

As well as being large, the house was also surrounded on all sides by vast gardens – lawns and terraces, fountains and features, flowers and trees stretched out all around it. It was, the old couple knew, an ideal place for children to play, so they didn't mind the local children sneaking in through the gates or over the walls. In fact, they encouraged it. They loved to hear the sounds of youth, to see the children running and hiding and having fun.

The children had come to understand that the old man and woman who lived in the house were very happy for them to play there. The old couple never interfered with the children's games, but they would walk out on to the main terrace, which was close to the house, and leave there an

ornate silver tray laden with sweets. The children would help
themselves to the sweets and, when they were all gone and
the tray was empty, one of the children would carry it back
to the house and rap loudly on the door with the heavy brass
door knocker. The more nervous of the children would
simply leave the silver tray by the door and run away; but the
braver ones would wait to hand the tray to the old man or
woman and say thank you. Then, all the children would wait
and watch whoever had come to collect the tray return it to
its place on a table in the drawing room; the table was close
to one of the main windows, to the right of the front door.

But then, one day, there were no sweets.

One of the more courageous children, a boy called
Tarmin, crept up to the house and peered through the
drawing-room window. He could see the old woman sitting
inside – she was all alone. She looked up and spotted Tarmin
at the window. For a moment, she seemed surprised, then her
expression slowly changed into a sad smile. She held Tarmin's
gaze for several seconds before looking away again. Even
from outside the window, Tarmin was sure she was crying.

A week later, the old woman was also gone.

In silence, the children watched a hearse drive slowly
out through the gates in front of the house. Inside lay the old
woman's body – the hearse was carrying her to be laid to rest
with her husband.

Somehow it didn't seem right to play in the gardens
without the old man and the old woman looking on. The
children came to the gardens less and less, and the grounds
of the house became overgrown and neglected.

A year after the old woman had died, some of the

children returned to the gates in front of the house. In the time since they had last played there, the house and its gardens had become a place to be avoided. Several children had gone to play in the gardens, and none of them had been seen since – it was as if they had vanished into the air.

'That's just stories,' one of the boys by the gate said. His name was Hal. 'They probably moved away.'

Some of the others agreed, but many didn't.

'I wish we could play in there again,' a girl called Izmay said. 'Can't we sneak in and see if it's safe?'

'Do you want to go in there?' Hal asked. 'Alone?'

Izmay shivered at the thought.

'Didn't think so,' said Hal. 'You're scared.'

'Aren't you?' Izmay said.

'I'm too old to play in gardens,' Hal replied, dodging the question. In truth he was just as scared as any of them.

'Don't tease her,' Tarmin told Hal.

'I'll go,' Izmay said suddenly. 'Into the garden. Right up to the house. You may be scared, but I'm not.'

Tarmin looked at her. Izmay was one of his best friends. What if the stories were true? What if she never came back? He couldn't bear the thought of never seeing her again. So he said, 'I'll come with you.'

Hal sneered. 'I bet you won't. I bet you'll just climb over the wall, hide for a bit and then come back. You won't go up to the house at all.'

'Yes we will,' Izmay insisted. 'We'll prove it too.'

'How?' Hal demanded.

Izmay frowned. She had no idea – but Tarmin did. 'The silver tray the old man and woman used to put out

with sweets on it,' he said. 'It was always on the table in the
drawing room, near the window.'

'What about it?' Hal asked.

'We'll go into the house and bring it back to show you,'
Tarmin told him.

'That's right,' Izmay agreed. 'Then you'll know we've
been right up to the house – right *inside* the house.'

'I suppose,' Hal said.

Hal said nothing more until Tarmin and Izmay were
being helped by the other children to climb the wall. He
watched them, biting his lip nervously even though he was
not going over the wall himself. 'You're really going in there?'
he asked at last.

Tarmin reached down from where he sat, perched on top
of the high wall, and pulled Izmay up next to him. 'Of course
we are.'

'You don't have to,' Hall said, speaking quickly. 'I was
just teasing. It could be dangerous. What if something really
did happen to the others in there? What if it happens to you?'

'Then I guess we won't be coming back,' Izmay told him.

'And if we don't come back,' Tarmin added, 'make sure
no one else follows us – ever. All right?'

'All right,' Hal said. 'Good luck,' he added, as Tarmin
grabbed hold of the branch of a tree and started to climb
down into the garden. Like the children waiting on the other
side of the wall, Tarmin thought that it would not be long
before he and Izmay were clambering back over the wall,
laughing with relief and brandishing the silver tray.

The gardens that they had once known so well were
now barely recognisable. Just as they had done many times

in the past, Tarmin and Izmay climbed down the trees –
but, instead of stepping down on to a clear patch of ground
as they used to, they now found themselves standing in an
overgrown tangle of grass and bracken.

They had climbed over the wall into a small wooded
area that had once opened out on to a wide lawn of closely
mown grass. Now, as they pushed their way through the
damp vegetation, they discovered that the grass was up to
their knees; it brushed against their legs as they walked, cold
and wet. They could see the house in the distance. It rose up
above them on the terrace but, while it used to look friendly
and inviting, it now seemed dark and forbidding.

Beyond the overgrown lawn was a formal garden with a
fountain at the centre. As they reached it, Tarmin and Izmay
stared at the unruly flower beds, the weeds spilling out across
the narrow stone pathways. The fountain – which had once
gushed clear, fresh, gurgling water – was now silent and dry.
Its plinth was weathered and chipped.

'It's so sad seeing it all like this,' Izmay said. 'I wish we
hadn't come.'

Tarmin agreed. 'Do you want to go back?' he asked.

Izmay shook her head. 'No. We should finish what we
started. Let's get to the house, find the tray and then get out
of here.'

The two children followed the path through the formal
garden. As they reached the end of the path they noticed
something beneath the canopy of a willow tree. There,
hidden under the branches which dipped low and cast deep
shadows, stood a dark figure.

Izmay gasped and clutched at Tarmin's arm. Tentatively

they stepped closer . . . and saw it was just a statue.

'I don't remember that being here before,' Tarmin said.

The statue was made of stone that was as weathered as the fountain had been; moss and lichen encrusted its lower half. The statue was an angel with her wings drawn up behind her. She held her face buried in her hands, as if she was weeping.

'Perhaps she's sad to see what's happened to the gardens,' Izmay said.

The two children continued on past the angel, and Tarmin turned to watch her as they went. *There is something unsettling about that angel,* he thought – but then he reminded himself that it was just a statue. He shook his head, trying to dismiss his own nervousness.

As they reached the end of the formal garden, Izmay took Tarmin's hand. Together, they started up the steps to the main terrace. When they were near the top, Tarmin looked back one more time. He could still see the statue beneath the tree – from here, it was barely more than a silhouette – but, instead of crying into her hands, the angel had looked up. She was staring at Tarmin and Izmay.

Tarmin hesitated, his foot frozen between steps – but then Izmay tugged at his hand, and he turned away. *It's just your imagination,* he told himself. *Imagination and fear. It's nothing more than a statue.*

Tarmin and Izmay reached the top of the steps, and discovered several more of the stone angels on the terrace. The statues seemed to have been positioned haphazardly, without any thought for how they might look. One was weeping into her hands, and another stared through blank

eyes across the terrace at the children. A third was barely more than a shadow in an alcove, while a fourth reached out towards them.

'This is strange,' Izmay said. 'Who put all these statues here?'

'Not just here,' Tarmin told her. He pointed out across the gardens. From where they stood on the raised terrace, they had a good view across the overgrown lawn and the formal garden – they could see right across to the wooded area in one direction and the lake in the other. Even from this distance, they could tell that the surface of the once-clear lake was a mass of algae and matted weeds. Dotted amongst the tall grass, in the shadows of the trees and around the edge of the lake, there were more of the angel statues.

'There are so many of them,' Izmay said. She shivered even though it was not an especially cold day. 'Do you find them frightening?'

Tarmin nodded. 'Let's see if we can find a way inside. We need to get the silver tray and leave.'

They turned back towards the house.

The statues on the terrace behind them had moved. There was no doubt about it this time. The angel that had been weeping was now staring up at them; the one in the shadows of the alcove had moved forward into brilliant sunshine; and the angel that had been reaching out towards them had shifted from where it had stood on the other side of the terrace. Now, it was right in front of them.

Izmay gasped, and drew her hand to her mouth. Tarmin grabbed her other hand and pulled her after him. They skirted round the statues, keeping well clear of them, and ran

towards the main door to the house. Tarmin did not
look back until they reached the door; when he did, the
angels had turned again – all of them were now staring
blankly at Tarmin and Izmay.

Izmay was already pushing open the door – by some
miracle, it was not locked. The two children almost fell
over the threshold and Tarmin slammed the door shut
behind them.

'Those statues –' Izmay gasped.

'If they are statues,' Tarmin said.

'They can *move*.'

Tarmin nodded. Izmay was right, but it was odd that
they had not actually seen the statues move. 'It's like they only
move when we're not looking,' he said.

'I –' Izmay bit her lip. 'I don't like it.'

'Nor do I,' Tarmin admitted. 'We just need to find the
tray, then we run back to the wall – as fast as we can.'

Izmay agreed. 'Which way, do you think?' she said.

Neither of them had ever been inside the house before.
They were in an entrance hall which had several doors
leading off it and ended in a wide flight of stairs that rose
to the upper floor. Tarmin pointed to a door on the right.
'That must be the drawing room,' he said. 'The table they
always put the tray on was by the window on that side of the
front door.'

They eased the door open. The room was lit only by the
light that filtered through the grimy windows. Dust hung in
the air like a thin mist, and rose in small clouds when they
trod on the carpet. As they entered the room, a weak beam of
sunlight gleamed on the tarnished silver of the tray – it was

lying on a table close to the nearest window.

'There it is!' Izmay dashed across to the table. She reached out for the tray – and screamed.

Tarmin was at her side in a moment, following her horrified gaze.

There, at the window, was a face. Pressed close against the glass, the face of an angel looked in at them. Its mouth was open wide, revealing long, sharp teeth, and the face itself was contorted in an expression that was a combination of anger, hunger and a snarl of triumph.

'Come on,' Tarmin urged. He grabbed the tray.

As one, the children backed away from the window, keeping their eyes fixed on the grotesque face staring back at them. Only when he finally turned did Tarmin see the danger – hidden behind the door through which they had entered the room was another statue. Another angel. Izmay, who was still backing away from the face at the window, had not seen it.

The statue behind the door had its hand stretched out, reaching for Izmay. Tarmin yelled a warning and Izmay began to turn.

Something cracked against the window, and Tarmin glanced away – just for a moment, the blink of an eye – but, when he turned back to the doorway, Izmay was gone.

The angel stared back at Tarmin, impassive, silent, still.

'Where is she?' Tarmin yelled at the statue. 'What have you done with her?'

Of course, the statue did not reply.

When Tarmin called out to her, Izmay looked round in surprise – but Tarmin was gone. And that wasn't the only thing that had changed.

Izmay was still in the same place, standing close to the drawing-room door, but everything was different – the furniture looked newer, the carpet less threadbare. Where just moments ago there had been dust and grime, now everything was sparkling and clean. The sun shone bright and unhindered through the clear glass of the windows.

'Tarmin!' Izmay called. 'Tarmin, where are you?'

A figure appeared in the doorway in front of her.

It was not Tarmin.

Tarmin pushed past the statue and out into the hall. He couldn't fathom how Izmay could have made her way through the door and out of the room in the fleeting moment that he had looked away from her – but where else could she be?

A sound – the slightest scrape of stone on wood – made him look back. The statue that had been in the drawing-room doorway was now right behind him, reaching out, its face twisted into a ferocious snarl. Tarmin jumped backwards.

Just for an instant, he felt the stone-cold touch of something grasping his shoulder.

Then, the world changed.

The dust vanished from the floor and the dirt disappeared from the windows. In the blink of an eye, everything in the house was gleaming and well cared for.

And, in front of Tarmin, stood Izmay. Beside her was an elderly man, who nodded and smiled as if he understood everything.

'Tarmin – you're here!' Izmay said, running over to

enfold him in a tight hug.

'Where else would I be?' he said, hugging her back. In truth, however, Tarmin was not entirely sure he knew where he was any more.

The old man led them back into the drawing room – it was so similar and yet so different to how it had been just moments ago. Through the windows, Tarmin and Izmay could see the gardens. They were no longer overgrown and neglected, but cared for and in good order. The grass was cut, the borders edged and there was no sign of any angel statues.

'It will take you a while to adjust,' the old man told them. 'It did me.'

Living inside the large house and looking out, rather than playing outside and occasionally looking in, did indeed take some time to get used to – but, gradually, Tarmin and Izmay became accustomed to it. They enjoyed each other's company, and they liked the old man, who so generously let them stay.

Though they never quite understood what had happened to the angels or how they had found themselves here, they were happy enough – which was fortunate because, not knowing how they had come to be in their present situation, they were not able to discover how to get back. There was nowhere else for them to go.

They would never learn how long the other children had waited for them on the other side of the garden wall. All they could do was hope that they had not been followed.

Slowly but surely the days became weeks, which in turn stretched into months and years. Tarmin grew into a handsome man, and Izmay a beautiful woman. When the creeping years finally claimed the old man, it seemed the most natural thing for the two friends to stay in the house. They continued to look after it and to care for the gardens they had loved to play in when they were young.

As they grew old together, Tarmin and Izmay didn't mind the local children sneaking in through the gates or over the walls to play in the gardens – in fact, they encouraged it. They loved to hear the sound of youth, to see the children running and hiding and having fun, just as they had once done.

It seemed to them there was only one thing missing. They hunted through the house, checking every cupboard and drawer, until one day Izmay found the ornate silver tray. She took it to Tarmin, and he agreed that it was perfect.

The next day, when the children came to play, Izmay and Tarmin covered the tray with sweets. Then, together, they walked out on to the terrace and, knowing the children were watching from behind the fountains and hidden among the trees, they left the tray on the ground.

They knew that once the children had eaten all the sweets there would be a knock at the front door. Then, when either Tarmin or Izmay answered it, one of the braver children might be waiting for them, ready to say thank you. Or there might just be the ornate silver tray, left on the ground close to the door.

FROZEN BEAUTY

nce upon a time, long before vortex drives and time capsules were even thought of, journeys through space took a very long time indeed. The distance between worlds was measured not in days or weeks, not in months or even years, but in centuries.

Some ships, like the great Leviathan fleet, were whole worlds in themselves. People lived, grew old and died in the artificial habitats on board these ships. Their children lived, grew old and died, and so did their children's children. Generations later, the ships would reach their new worlds.

But, on most ships, the crew and passengers slept for the centuries it took to reach their destination. So it was on the *Stellar Fire* – the most advanced ship of its age, the pride of the fleet of colony vessels. The *Stellar Fire*'s captain was renowned for her courage and her skill; she was hailed as one of the very best officers anywhere in the space fleet, and this was perhaps why she was given command of its finest and

fastest ship. She was as proud of her command as her crew
was to work for her.

But even the most advanced and prized of starships
encountered problems. The *Stellar Fire* was just fifty years into
her voyage, skirting the frontier worlds of the Andromeda
System, when her engines mis-phased, and the ship crashed
on to a small, uncharted planet. All contact was lost with the
main computers. The systems that were designed to wake the
crew in an emergency failed, and the sleepers slept on . . .

That might have been the end of the story, but for one
thing: the captain of the *Stellar Fire* had a brother. When
the ship had started its journey, he was no one special –
just a young man unimaginably proud of his older sister's
reputation and achievement. But, fifty years later, in his
twilight years, Abadon Glammis had become one of the
richest men in the galaxy – in any galaxy, come to that.

When he learned that all contact had been lost with
his sister's ship, he immediately organised a rescue mission.
He did not know what had happened to the *Stellar Fire*, and
he had no clue as to whether or not his sister had survived.
Deep down, he had always understood that he would never
see her again – but, in spite of that, she was still his sister and
he loved her dearly. He felt his heart could not rest if he did
not at least try to find her.

The crew of the rescue ship slept in cryogenic caskets
for most of their journey, just as the *Stellar Fire*'s crew had
done. The captain of the rescue ship had been chosen for his
determination and energy as much as his skill and experience.
He was young, but he was already one of the most experienced
officers in the fleet. He had piloted a ship round the Horns of

Angular and made the Neglev Run a record five times.

One of the reasons this captain was so successful was that he always ensured he understood his ship. He made sure he knew its strengths and also its limitations – where he could trust the technology, and where he needed to keep a close watch on it. He trusted the ship's systems to scan every planet close to where the *Stellar Fire* had vanished. He trusted the systems to wake him when they found something – if they ever found something. If not, he might well sleep forever.

Back on the captain's home world, time passed and, all the while, he slept and his ship searched. Abadon Glammis grew old and died. Slowly, the fate of the *Stellar Fire* and of the ship sent to find her faded from memory and into legend.

It was another hundred years before the rescue ship's detectors finally found a trace – just the tiniest suggestion – of what might be the remains of the *Stellar Fire*. The rescue ship's captain was awoken. He blinked the ice from his eyes, and felt the frost slowly melt from his cheeks. He yawned and stretched, and set in motion the sequence that would revive the rest of his crew. A glance at the instruments was enough to convince him that they had indeed found what they were looking for: the *Stellar Fire*. But would anyone have survived the crash?

The rescue ship lowered itself through the atmosphere and towards the small, unsurveyed planet. The world was covered in dense forest, and the nearest clearing in which the ship could put down was several miles from the crashed remains of the *Stellar Fire*. The darkness of this thickly wooded planet seemed safe enough. And so it would have been, if that was all that awaited them outside their ship.

Before they headed out into the forest, the captain
assembled his crew.

'No one knows what lies in this forest,' he warned them.
'We have our survival suits and our laser blasters. We are
trained and equipped for anything we might encounter. But
I cannot order you to follow me. I can only ask that, having
come this far, you agree to accompany me the last few miles.'

Many of the crew had served with the captain before,
and those who had not knew his reputation; they would
go through anything if he asked them. Every one of them
agreed to follow him.

'I do not know what we shall find at the crash site,' he
admitted. 'It may be that the ship was totally destroyed and
everyone perished in the impact. It is possible that we have
spent over a hundred years asleep for nothing. But, until we
reach the crash site, we won't know. We may discover that
our journey has not been in vain – if we can rescue just one
survivor from the *Stellar Fire*, then a century of frozen slumber
is worth it.'

And so they set out through the forest. The way was
dark and treacherous, with many hazards. Long creepers
hung down through the foliage like the legs of huge spiders,
and some of the plants hissed and spat at the humans as they
passed. Sharp, thorny tendrils swiped at them; wild animals
growled from the shadows, but were too afraid to approach
these strange creatures who had descended from the sky into
their world. At one point, a great chasm opened up across
the landscape in front of them, and they had to fashion ropes
from the hanging creepers to swing themselves across.

Night and day were lost beneath the heavy canopy

of strange plants and alien vegetation. The crew camped when they grew weary, and the captain set a watch in case the animals hiding in the shadows should get too curious. But, as the crew got gradually closer to the site where the *Stellar Fire* had crashed, the growls of the animals quietened and eventually disappeared altogether. It was as though the animals knew of some greater danger ahead, and they didn't dare follow the humans into it.

When the crew had rested, they moved on, all keen to find the *Stellar Fire* and – they hoped – its passengers and crew. The captain felt anticipation growing inside him as his navigation handset assured him they were closing on their destination. He had heard and read so much about the lost ship's captain, and he could not wait to see the great ship she had commanded – and maybe even meet her in person.

And then, finally, they saw it.

The great metal hull of the *Stellar Fire* appeared through the orange and yellow leaves and stems in front of them. Dappled sunlight shone on its corroded sides. Multicoloured vegetation had grown up through the hull itself – plants with sharp, narrow leaves and studded with powerful suckers clung to every surface. The forest had claimed the ship for itself.

The crew found the main hatchway. It was partly buried in the ground, and matted over with vines and clawing roots – but it had been torn open. Something had already forced its way inside.

Cautiously, the captain led his team through the hatch. It looked like the ship's systems were still running on emergency power, as the whole interior was bathed in a dull red glow. They made their way through the shattered remains of corridors and walkways, past storerooms and cargo holds, towards the cryogenic section, where the passengers and crew were sleeping – or so they hoped. They hacked their way through the trees and plants that had grown everywhere. Shadows loomed and deepened around them. They heard something scuttle away from them and into the gloom. The captain had been growing increasingly unsettled, but now he was certain: something was following them through the broken remains of the *Stellar Fire*.

At last, the crew reached the sleeping passengers. They were in vast cryogenic chambers, laid out inside frozen caskets, preserved through the years. Sleeping . . . or dead. As the captain moved slowly through the chambers, he realised the terrible truth: some of the caskets had failed, and the occupants had aged to death in their sleep. Yet other caskets were smashed open, the sleepers inside gone. In one casket, a sticky, glutinous mass of green writhed and pulsed. As the captain and his crew looked on, it heaved itself over the edge of the smashed lid, and squelched down on to the floor.

It was like nothing the captain had ever seen before. But, thanks to the briefing implants he had taken before the journey, he knew what it was: the larva of an Andromedan parasite. His implants detailed the creature's life cycle, and spelled out the threat it posed. Without hesitation, the captain drew his laser blaster and opened fire. In moments the creature was dead, a slimy mess across the floor of the chamber.

'What was that?' asked one of the members of the rescue team, her voice taut with nerves.

'A Wirrn grub,' the captain answered. He told them
how the massive maggot-like creatures devoured sleeping
passengers, absorbing not just their flesh but also their minds,
memories and experiences too. 'They lay eggs inside us,'
he explained. 'Any casket that is not still sealed could contain
a Wirrn, growing and ready to hatch out at any moment.'

The captain and his crew had no idea how many adult
Wirrn they faced. But the captain knew that their strength
lay just as much in numbers as in their laser blasters; they
needed to awaken any survivors and escape back to their
own ship. Soon the Wirrn, fearful of losing their food supply,
would attack.

The captain and his crew moved back to the central area
between all the doorways to the cryogenic chambers, and the
captain set guards at the entrances to each of them. Pointing
to a control panel set into the ship's wall, he ordered his
technician to begin the revival process.

The scuttling of the Wirrn seemed to be growing louder.
The captain imagined dozens of the adult creatures, like huge
upright insects, massing to attack them. Soon the crew would
have to fight their way out – and the sooner the better, before
the Wirrn were prepared.

'How long?' the captain demanded of his technician.

The technician shook his head. 'The systems are
damaged. I can prime the revival process to start, but the
revival systems on each casket aren't working. We need the
ship's main computer to trigger the awakening.'

The captain immediately saw the problem. 'The computer
will need a command access code,' he said.

The technician nodded. 'There's only one person who

will know this ship's code: its captain. We *have* to revive her. *Somehow.*'

'We have to find her first,' the captain said. The ship's officers were not kept with the passengers; they would be sleeping in a sealed compartment closer to the main control deck. If the Wirrn had not already reached them, that was.

The blast of a laser split the silence. A wounded Wirrn scuttled back from one of the chamber doorways. It was obvious now that the captain and his crew would have to fight their way out of the area they were in. Leaving half of his team to guard the sleeping passengers, the captain assembled the others and gave them their orders.

The first challenge was to escape from the cryogenic section and into the main ship. There were Wirrn at every doorway now, lurking in the shadows and biding their time. There was no doubt they would strike when they could.

One young man ventured too close to a doorway; the long forelimbs of a Wirrn snaked out from the shadows, wrapped tightly round the man and began dragging him away. Only the quick response of his comrades saved him – one grabbed his legs while another blasted at the Wirrn's body until it released its grip. On the captain's order, the rescue team opened fire again, blasting into the shadows and driving the monstrous creatures back. They scurried away, screeching in pain and fear and anger.

The journey through the ship was a red-lit nightmare. Barbed plants whipped at them as they ran. Branches blocked their way. Ivy and creepers laced the floor and threatened to snare and trip them at every step. And Wirrn waited in the shadows – they reached out for any stragglers, hoping to pick

them off. The rescuers fired at any movement, any shadow
that seemed too deep and dark, any hint of the creatures.

They came across a whole section of the ship's floor
that had been slowly ripped away by the forest as it forced
its way inside the *Stellar Fire*. The captain led the way across,
clambering up the trunk of a tree and out along its branches
until he could drop down on the other side. His feet clanged
against the metal floor. A tentacle whipped out from a
doorway, wrapping itself round his ankle and pulling him
down. As he fell, he jabbed his laser blaster into the dark
shape that was dragging him across the floor. The sound of
the shot echoed around the metal structure, and was only
drowned out by the piercing shriek of the dying Wirrn.

At every corner, they hesitated, checked for the creatures,
then moved cautiously on. At every dark doorway, they
glanced apprehensively ahead, expecting a ferocious Wirrn to
hurl itself at them. With every step, they grew closer to their
goal: the forward section of the ship, where they would find
the control deck and the crew's cryogenic chamber – and,
they hoped, the ship's sleeping captain.

The journey seemed to take forever, but finally they stood
in front of the door to an official-looking chamber. It had to
be the crew's. Each and every one of them held their breath
as the captain activated the opening mechanism and the door
slid slowly open. The door groaned and protested, grown
stubborn with age and the branches that had forced their way
round and through it. It opened just enough for the captain
to force his way through and into the chamber beyond.

The caskets inside were bathed in a pale blue light, a
contrast to the blood red that had lit the rest of the ship.

Here, it was cold and stark by comparison. The captain looked across the chamber, taking in the row of glass-topped caskets in front of him. He let out a sigh of relief, his breath misting in the air. The caskets appeared intact.

'It doesn't look as if the Wirrn have got this far into the ship,' the technician said. 'The air is colder here. This chamber has not been disturbed.'

The captain was already walking along the row of caskets, looking for the ship's sleeping captain. But could they wake her when they found her? One casket stood apart from the others, slightly raised, as befits the senior officer on a ship. The captain knelt beside this casket. He wiped his gloved hand across the glass surface of its lid. It was thick with frost, but he managed to clear a space to see down into the casket – to see the woman lying sleeping inside. She looked so peaceful, so still. So beautiful. One look at her face, glistening with a sheen of ice, and the captain knew he had found the woman he was looking for. He had to save her.

Suddenly, he saw a movement. For a moment, he thought that she was waking, that her eyelids had fluttered impossibly into life. But then he realised that what he had seen was a reflection in the glass – the movement of the creature behind him.

A yell of warning came at the same moment as the captain realised his mistake. He threw himself sideways, and the Wirrn's tentacles sliced through the air where he had been kneeling just seconds before. The creature's tentacles clattered against the glass casket, sending up a shower of frosted particles that hung in the air as an icy cloud.

The Wirrn turned back to the captain. He saw his own

reflection now, distorted in the huge eyes of the creature as it lunged at him once more. He raised his gun and there was a brilliant flash of light. The Wirrn was blasted backwards, dead before it hit the ground.

'Can you wake her?' the captain asked the technician, who was busying himself at the casket's controls.

'I can shut down the cryogenics and restore her body to its correct temperature,' the technician told him. 'But, without the command code to activate the revival process, it is up to the woman herself to begin to breathe.' The technician set the controls. 'Now all we can do is wait.'

And so they waited. The ice in the casket began to thaw. Cold mist rose from inside. Slowly the frosted sheen on the woman's face dissolved to water, and ran like tears down her cheeks. But her eyes remained closed, and she did not draw breath.

'Wirrn!' a voice called from the doorway. But the captain barely heard. All his attention was focused on the woman lying asleep in the casket. All his thoughts were about her frozen beauty.

'Now,' the technician whispered as he checked the controls. 'She has to breathe *now*. If not, she will never wake.'

With the sound of blaster fire echoing around the room, and the screeches of the wounded and dying Wirrn ringing in his ears, the captain leaned down into the casket. He pressed his lips against the woman's and breathed his own breath into her lungs, willing her to wake up.

Nothing.

He tried again – the kiss of life. And, this time, the woman's chest heaved in a sudden, startled response.

Her eyes opened, and she drew in great rasping breaths of the frosty air.

The captain helped her out of the casket. He shrugged out of his jacket and draped it over her shoulders to keep her warm while she recovered from her long, cold sleep. Then, as she sat shivering, he explained who he and his crew were, why they had come and what they had found. As the two captains spoke, the technician worked at a console, accessing the main computer. By the time he was ready, the newly woken captain had recovered. She keyed in the command code that she had learned so many years ago, back before her long journey had begun.

Behind them, the other caskets slowly started to thaw. Their lids sprang open. Helped by the processes activated by the command code, the sleepers inside took their first tentative breaths. Deep within the ship, the caskets in the other cryogenic chambers were also opening. Slowly but surely, the temperature in the crew's chamber began to rise. Slowly but surely, the *Stellar Fire* was coming back to life.

The remaining sleepers awoke, and the captain and his crew armed them with laser blasters from the ship's armoury. Together, the two crews fought their way through the Wirrn, and the Wirrn retreated. They were outnumbered and knew they could not stand against the blaster fire. The two captains led the way out of the ship – the woman who had slept for so very long, and the man who had come to wake her. Together they led their people – crew, passengers and rescuers – out into the forest.

It was a slow journey back to the rescue ship, but their spirits were high. As they walked through the trees, the planet's distant sun slowly rose above the forest's canopy. Light shone down, pale and filtered. For the sleepers of the Stellar Fire, this was a new dawn, a new beginning.

As they reached the rescue ship, the woman turned to the captain who had woken her. She took his hands in hers. 'Thank you,' she said. And his smile was as beautiful to her as her sleeping, frozen beauty had been to him.

CINDERELLA
AND THE
MAGIC BOX

espite being one of the prettiest girls in the kingdom, Cinderella was also one of the unluckiest. When she was very young, her mother had caught a fever and died. Her father grieved for several years, but eventually fell in love again. His new wife was a widow who had two daughters a little older than Cinderella.

They all lived together happily – or so Cinderella thought – in the grand house where Cinderella had grown up. However, when her father took ill and died not long after marrying his new wife, things swiftly changed. Cinderella's stepmother inherited the house and all her husband's wealth, and it soon became clear that the woman and her daughters had only wanted Cinderella's father's money and possessions. There was certainly no love in their hearts for Cinderella, and she suspected there had never been any love in their hearts for her father either.

They did not throw Cinderella out of her own home –

although perhaps it might have been kinder if they had. Instead, they made her cook and wash for them. She cleaned and polished, did the shopping in the town, prepared the meals, tidied and did all the housework.

Cinderella's stepmother and stepsisters made her do everything for them, but there always remained one thing they could not make her do and that was be unhappy. No matter how hard she had to work or how cruelly she was treated, Cinderella was always smiling. Yes, she knew she had been unlucky – she had lost both her parents at a very young age, and was now treated little better than a slave – but Cinderella was grateful to have a roof over her head and enough to eat. She knew there were many in her world who were still less fortunate than she was.

Nonetheless, there were also many who were more fortunate. From the kitchen window, Cinderella could see the castle where the lords and ladies lived perched on the hill behind the town. Taking a moment's break from the filthy dishes she was made to scrub morning and night, she would often gaze through the window and wonder what it was like inside the castle. Occasionally, she would catch a glimpse of Lord Darke's carriage passing through the town on its way to or from the castle – the blinds were always drawn, and Lord Darke himself was rarely seen.

The years passed, and Cinderella grew into a young woman. Beneath the grime and dirt, the soot and dust that always coated her face, she was far more beautiful than either of her rather plain stepsisters. They hated and resented her all the more for it.

Once every year, the most handsome men and beautiful

women in the town were invited to a ball at the castle. If her father had still been alive, Cinderella liked to think she herself might have been invited. She might even have been one of the few who were chosen to stay in the castle and live out their days there in luxury. Although she would not have wanted to leave her parents if they had still been alive, now she would happily exchange her life at home for one in Lord Darke's household.

At last, one day, an invitation to the masked ball at Lord Darke's castle was delivered. Cinderella's jealous stepsisters did their best to keep it a secret from her – they did not want her to go because they knew that her beauty would certainly outshine them both.

It wasn't long, though, before Cinderella learned of the ball. It was the only thing the people in the market were talking about when she went to buy the meat and vegetables.

'Surely you'll be going,' Bunton, the butcher's lad, said to her. 'All the young men and women are invited, as well as the most important people in the town.'

'Everyone except me,' Cinderella told him. She felt the little happiness and hope she still had inside her ebbing away.

The ball was to celebrate the visit of the prince of Arbesk. The province of Arbesk had been a rival to Lord Darke's realm for as long as anyone could recall. Bunton told Cinderella that the prince's visit was supposed to be a gesture of goodwill and peace between the two provinces, but Cinderella could tell from Bunton's expression that he was not convinced.

'I've met Lord Darke,' he told her. 'When I deliver the meat to the castle, he is sometimes there. I've only ever seen

him in the evening – they say he does not venture out in
daylight. I've noticed how he treats the servants, and there's
something in his eyes . . .' Bunton shuddered at the memory.
'I don't know what it is, but it frightens me. They say he eats
his meat raw, the blood still dripping from it.'

When she returned from the market, Cinderella
asked her stepmother about the ball. The cruel woman
just laughed.

'It is not for the likes of you,' she said.

'I thought all the young people were invited,' Cinderella said.

'It is only for important people,' her stepmother replied,
drawing herself up to her full height. 'People like me and
my daughters.'

'You are going?' Cinderella was not surprised – as well as
his wealth, her stepmother had inherited her father's position
in society.

'I am,' her stepmother replied proudly. 'It is a great
honour. Lord Darke has finally realised how much my family
and I contribute to the community. You –' she added with a
cruel smile – 'are not my family. You will stay here and clean
the entire house from top to bottom. You will polish the silver
and sweep out the backyard.'

On the day of the ball, Cinderella's stepmother
presented her with a list of the work she must complete by the
time they returned from the ball. Before she started, though,
Cinderella had to help her stepsisters to get ready. She fitted
them into their lavish dresses, all the while wishing she had a
dress just half as fine for herself. She braided and arranged
their hair, wishing she had the time – and a good reason –
to do her own. Finally, she watched them climb, along with

their mother, into the carriage which bore her father's coat of arms on the door. The driver smiled sympathetically at Cinderella – he had known her since she was a child, and had worked for her father. Then he twitched the reins and the carriage drove off towards Lord Darke's castle. As it disappeared into the gathering night, Cinderella heard the castle clock chime eight.

Back inside the house, Cinderella was just starting to mop the kitchen floor when she felt a draught on the back of her neck. It ruffled her hair and made her shiver. Thinking she must have left a window open, she started to cross the room to check, but was interrupted by a strange noise, which split the air – a wheezing, grinding, scraping sound. Cinderella watched in amazement as a blue box manifested in the corner of the kitchen. She stared at it in disbelief for several moments before the front opened and a man stepped out.

The man smiled at Cinderella. He flicked a wayward lock of hair from his eye, but it flopped straight back to where it had been. This time he ignored it.

'Who are you?' Cinderella asked. She wondered who would travel in such a strange and exciting manner, and a thought occurred to her. 'You're not the prince of Arbesk, are you?'

The man's smile expanded into a grin. 'The prince of Arbesk will be up at the castle, enjoying the masked ball, by now,' he said. 'Which is exactly where you should be.'

Cinderella shook her head sadly. 'I'm not invited.'

'Of course you're invited. In fact, you are the most important guest of all,' the man told her.

Cinderella laughed at this. 'Me? I don't even have a dress to wear. They'd never let me in like this.' She gestured at her tattered dress and smudged apron. One of her worn-down shoes had a hole in the end of it, from which a lonely toe poked. She certainly was a sorry sight.

The strange man raised his eyebrows. He walked over to her, took the mop she was holding and threw it across the room. 'You do need a bit of work,' he agreed. 'Come on then.'

'Come on where?' Cinderella asked.

'Into my magic box,' the man told her. 'You can have a quick bath, and I'll find some clothes for you to choose from.'

Cinderella was a little nervous, but she thought the man, though a bit strange, seemed trustworthy. Plus, she'd much rather go to the ball than be stuck scrubbing the kitchen floor. So she followed him through the door into his blue box.

She had expected it to be no bigger than a cupboard – which is how big it appeared from the outside – but, once inside, it opened out into a whole mansion, larger than her own house. It was perhaps even larger than Lord Darke's castle. The man led her through a large chamber with a strange table in the middle of it, and down corridors and walkways until eventually he ushered her through a door and into the most magnificent bathroom she had ever seen.

'Just ring when you're done,' he said, and showed Cinderella a bell pull hanging close to the enormous bath. 'The left tap is cold water, the right tap is hot water and the middle one is lemonade,' he told her. 'You probably won't need the lemonade, but if you want bubbles there's a switch just there. I've put the time lock on, so take as long as you like.

It'll still be half past eight when you finish.'

The man left, and Cinderella had the most luxurious bath of her life. She took her time, then dried herself on the softest towel she had ever used. Finally she put on a loose bathrobe, and tugged the bell pull.

'Brilliant,' said the man, when he appeared moments later. 'Next stop: the wardrobe.'

Cinderella had never seen so many clothes. There were whole rooms full of them. The man had already picked out several dresses that he thought she might like; he also showed her a whole rack of other dresses she could try, and then he left her to it.

It took a while, but Cinderella finally found the perfect blue, billowing dress. When the man returned, he nodded and straightened his rather floppy bow tie. 'I know just the right shoes to go with it,' he told her.

The shoes he offered were made of crystal. The toes were faceted so that they caught the light and shone like cut diamonds. 'Are they made of glass?' Cinderella wondered aloud.

'Shoes made of glass? That wouldn't be very safe,' the man said. 'They're actually midnight crystal. Much tougher than glass and, thanks to a clear polymer lining that adapts to the shape of your foot, a lot softer too. Glass shoes would just be silly.'

Cinderella put the shoes on. She was surprised at how comfortable they were and how well they fitted.

'There's just one other thing you need,' the man told her. He produced what looked like a metal wand.

'What's that?' Cinderella asked.

'Sonic screwdriver,' he told her.

'And why do I need it?' she said.

'You need it,' the man said, 'so that at exactly midnight, when the castle clock chimes the first note of the hour, you can do this.' He showed her how to press a button that made the end of the wand glow. 'Can you do that?'

Cinderella nodded. It seemed easy enough. 'But why?'

The man looked surprised. 'Didn't I explain? It's to save your life. Right then – time we were going.'

As she followed the man back along the corridors and walkways, Cinderella wondered how she was going get to the castle in her long dress and wearing shoes that were made of something that wasn't glass. But, when they stepped out of his blue box, she found that they were already there – the box was now, somehow, standing right next to a side door of the castle.

'Good luck,' the man said, and he shook Cinderella's hand. 'Remember – exactly midnight. No sooner, and certainly no later. Then come back here. I'll give you a lift home.'

'But aren't you coming to the ball as well?' she asked.

The man shook his head. 'They'd spot me at once. Probably smell the artron energy as soon as I stepped inside the castle. That's why I need you to use the sonic screwdriver.'

The man told Cinderella how to find her way from the side door through to the main ballroom. 'Have fun,' he told her. 'Don't forget – midnight on the dot. Oh, and you'll need this too.' He handed her an ornate mask fixed to a short stick, which Cinderella could hold in front of her face. 'It is a masked ball, after all.'

Cinderella was afraid that someone would stop her and demand to know what she was doing there. What if her stepmother saw her? She held the mask close to her face, and hurried through the castle.

Cinderella heard the sound of music and laughter long before she saw the flickering candlelight. The ballroom, when she eventually reached it, was full of people drinking wine and talking. In the middle of the room, people danced while a small orchestra played music. At the far end, beyond the dance floor, was a raised platform; here, looking down upon their guests, sat Lord and Lady Darke. They did not wear masks, although the other people seated on the platform did. Lord Darke was tall with thin, lean features and black hair swept back from his forehead. Lady Darke's hair was just as black but hung, straight and elegant, to below her shoulders. There was something cold, Cinderella thought, about their eyes.

Although she did her best to stay inconspicuous as she enjoyed the music and sipped a glass of wine, Cinderella grew increasingly aware that people were staring at her. Despite their masks, she could tell who most of them were. She tried not to meet their eyes, hoping that no one would recognise her – but it was a man she was sure she had never seen before who came and spoke to her. He was dressed in an elegant suit and wore a plain white mask with a pattern of gold swirls across it. He stood next to her as she watched the dancers, and said, 'Forgive me, but you seem rather ill at ease.'

He seemed pleasant and, since Cinderella was sure she did not know him, she confessed that she was confused as to why people kept staring at her. The man seemed both

surprised and amused by this. 'You really don't know?'
he asked.

Cinderella shook her head. The man gently took her
hand, and said, 'Dance with me, and then I shall tell you.'

It was years since Cinderella had danced. When her
father was alive, he had made sure that she had dancing
lessons every week; now she was amazed at how quickly
she remembered what to do. When the music paused, and
the dance was over, the man led Cinderella to the side of the
dance floor.

'You seem happier now,' he said, and indeed she was.
Her nervousness was gone and she had even stopped noticing
the way the other guests were watching her. She realised how
much she had enjoyed dancing with the masked stranger.

The evening wore on, and Lord and Lady Darke and
the others on the platform descended to join the dancers
on the floor. Cinderella danced again with the man she had
met. She wondered who he could be; he had not told her his
name, and she felt it would be rude to ask. In the end, her
answer came from the most unlikely of places.

As a new dance began, the stranger took Cinderella's
hand to lead her back on to the dance floor – but, before they
could start dancing, another figure stepped in front of them.
It was Lord Darke.

'You really cannot keep our most beautiful guest all for
yourself,' Lord Darke said to the man. Then he turned to
Cinderella. 'I think this may be the last dance. Will you share
it with me?'

Cinderella hesitated, noting again how icy his gaze was.

'I can assure you,' Lord Darke went on, his mouth

twisting into a thin smile, 'that I am every bit as accomplished a dancer as the prince of Arbesk.'

Cinderella gasped. Was that who she had been dancing with all this time? The prince bowed, and stepped back. Still shocked, Cinderella found herself being led on to the dance floor by Lord Darke. Beside them, Lady Darke took the prince's hand and led him out on to the dance floor too.

Lord Darke was indeed a good dancer, but Cinderella felt uneasy with him. Not only were his eyes cold, but his hands were like ice. As they danced, his attention seemed to be fixed on Cinderella's pale, slender neck. She hoped the dance would soon be over and she could perhaps return to the prince.

Cinderella was also aware that time was moving on – it must be almost midnight. Sure enough, at that moment, she heard the castle clock begin to chime. The sound was almost lost in the music, making it difficult to count the hours, but Cinderella knew it had to be midnight. She could feel the metal wand the strange man had given her tucked into a pocket inside one of her sleeves – but she couldn't reach it while Lord Darke held her hand in the dance.

As the clock continued to chime, Lord Darke's grip on Cinderella's hand grew even tighter and colder. Over his shoulder, Cinderella could see the prince dancing with Lady Darke. As she watched, it seemed that Lady Darke's eyes became deeper and blacker; then, when Lady Darke saw Cinderella watching her, she smiled. Her lips curled back to reveal long, sharp teeth beneath.

Suddenly, the music stopped. Someone screamed.

Across the room, Cinderella could see the people sitting

on the raised platform pulling off their masks. They were all smiling – and they all had long, sharp teeth protruding over their lower lips. Lord Darke's grip on Cinderella's hand tightened still further and he lowered his head towards her neck with a hiss of anticipation. She saw Lady Darke mirror his actions, her sharp teeth descending towards the prince's neck.

With a sudden, panicked fury, Cinderella tore herself free from Lord Darke. As the clock struck the final chime of midnight, she pulled the metal wand from her sleeve and fumbled for the button the man had shown her. She pressed it, and the tip lit up.

Lord Darke was advancing angrily towards Cinderella but, when he saw the glowing wand, he hesitated. His eyes widened in surprise and he stopped. Across the room, Lady Darke and the other nobles also froze. Slowly, Lady Darke put her hand to her face. The smooth, unblemished skin of her cheek was withering in front of Cinderella's eyes. The prince, who had also managed to break free from his dancing partner, backed away in horror as her cheeks hollowed and the skin across her face tightened like old parchment.

Lord Darke reached out towards Cinderella, stumbling forward and trying to grab the wand, but she held it high above her head. Lord Darke crumpled to his knees. He stared at Cinderella for a moment – his hair white, his face little more than a skull – then he pitched forwards. His clutching hand disintegrated into a pile of grey dust. Behind him, Lady Darke and the other nobles sank to their knees and also dissolved into dust.

For a moment there was silence. Cinderella turned off

the wand and slipped it back into the secret pocket in her sleeve. Guests screamed and ran from the ballroom, and amongst them, she spotted her stepmother and stepsisters pushing their way towards the exit. Cinderella hurried in the opposite direction, towards the passageway that would take her back to the side door and the man with his magic blue box.

She had no idea what had happened, only that she had to get away. In the back of her mind she was worried that she must get home before her stepmother and stepsisters did. She ran down a short flight of steps and, in her haste, twisted her foot. One of her shoes fell off, but she wasted no time stopping to pick it up – she simply took off the other shoe and ran in bare feet. Was it her imagination, or could she hear someone running after her?

Finally, she emerged into the cold night air. She stood, gasping for breath, beside the blue box. The door opened and the man came out. He was grinning. 'You did it then? Well done!'

She was so out of breath she could barely speak. 'What did I do?' she managed to ask at last.

'Oh, just a simple sonic resonance.' He took back the wand and slipped it into his jacket pocket. 'At just the right moment, as the vampires are changing, it can interfere with their molecular transformation and, well, you saw the effect. Who's your friend?'

It took Cinderella a moment to work out what he meant. She turned to see that the prince was coming out of the side door. He walked slowly over to Cinderella, and handed her the shoe she had lost.

'I don't know what you did,' he said, 'but I think you saved all of our lives.'

'She certainly did,' the strange man said. 'Especially yours. Lord Darke was going to turn you into a vampire so he could send you back to turn all the nobles of Arbesk into vampires too. This whole party was for your benefit.'

'I came here looking for peace,' said the prince quietly.

'I'm sorry you didn't find what you were looking for,' Cinderella told him.

The prince took her hands in his. 'It's all right. I found something much better.'

She frowned, confused. 'What do you mean?'

'I think,' the strange man beside her said, 'that he's asking you if you want to be a princess. So, I'll leave you to it then.'

Cinderella did not hear the door to the blue box close. She didn't notice the breeze that ruffled her hair, or the grating, rasping sound as the box slowly faded away. All her attention was focused on the prince whose life she had saved. It appeared that Cinderella's luck had finally changed for good.

THE TWINS
IN THE WOOD

nce, long ago but not so terribly far away, the emperor of Levithia lay dying. He was not an old man, but he had caught a fever and quickly became weaker and weaker. Before long it was evident that he did not have long left. The emperor's brother, Lord Grath, sat by his bedside as his life faded; the emperor's twin children, barely into their teenage years, were also close by.

Rigel, the emperor's most trusted advisor, visited often – and, in between visits, he ensured that the business of governing the empire continued smoothly despite the emperor's worsening condition. As the emperor's death drew closer, the empire's nobles and senior officials also gathered to be with their leader.

At last, the emperor drew his final breath. Lord Grath pulled a sheet up over his deceased brother's face. 'Rigel,' Grath said. 'Have the council gather at once. They must know immediately of the emperor's death, and they must appoint a regent to rule on behalf of the children until they come of age.'

Grath then sighed, and turned to the twins. The boy, Asher, was pale with grief; his sister, Ella, fought back her tears.

'You are both emperor now,' Grath told them. 'You shall rule together, just as you were born together. Whoever is appointed as regent will guide you and help you until you are old enough and capable of ruling on your own.'

Next, Grath turned to the emperor's physician. 'You must examine the body,' he said quietly. 'This illness struck quickly and has infected no one else. I should like to be sure that it was indeed misfortune that took my beloved brother from us, and not something more sinister.'

The council of Levithia convened that same day. They confirmed that Asher and Ella would rule jointly as the new emperor, and the council appointed their uncle, Lord Grath, as regent of Levithia. The twins might have had the title, but it was Grath who would have the power – at least for the next two years, until they came of age.

But the next two years was not long enough for Grath. When the emperor's physician determined that the emperor had died from poisoning, Grath seized his chance. While their father had been alive, the twins had kept to themselves – they did not take part in affairs of state, and had a reputation for being aloof and cold. In actual fact, they were simply quiet and happiest in their own company. It was not difficult for Lord Grath to paint them as ambitious and cruel, craving the emperor's throne for themselves and unwilling to wait for their father's natural death.

The only one in the council to speak up for the twins was Rigel, but such was Lord Grath's power and influence that Rigel himself was denounced. Rigel pointed out that the twins could not have obtained or administered the poison themselves – they were too young, too inexperienced. Lord Grath had an answer to that: they had been helped. And who was better placed to commit the actual crime than Rigel himself? Perhaps Rigel had felt that the emperor no longer paid him enough attention; perhaps he thought that the young twins would be easier to manipulate. Whatever the reason, it was clear – according to Grath – that Rigel had been the ringleader. Rigel was sentenced to execution, but he still had friends on the council and in the palace, and he slipped away before he could be arrested.

The twins, however, were not so lucky. They appeared before the council and, despite their tearful protestations of innocence, were found guilty of their father's murder. They too were sentenced to death.

Lord Grath watched with well-concealed satisfaction as the children were placed in an obliteration module. He feigned sadness as the hatch was closed and the countdown began. A large crowd gathered along with the council to watch as the obliteration module was launched from the surface of Levithia and started its journey into space and through the Seven Systems.

But at the point where the module was supposed to explode into a million fragments and kill its occupants instantly something went wrong. The obliteration module did not explode. It kept going. Inside, the two children huddled together, awaiting their death. They did not realise that their lives had been spared until they saw a planet appear through the module's only window. The module had entered the atmosphere of this planet, and the children were still alive.

The module burned down through the sky, and the inside grew hotter and hotter. Just as the twins felt they were about to burst into flame, just as they realised that they were doomed to die after all, the module ploughed into the planet's surface. It bounced and twisted, but mercifully remained intact. Eventually, it came to a halt. The final jolt, as the module struck a tree, jarred open the sealed hatchway, and the twins looked out in surprise at a clear orange sky framed by a canopy of trees.

Shaken and groggy, but glad to be alive, Asher and Ella clambered out of the module. They found themselves in a wood, but immediately surrounding them was the charred destruction their module had wreaked when it descended on the planet. For a long time they stood, holding hands, and looked around them. They had no idea where they were or what they should do.

'We'll need to find food,' Asher said at last.

'And shelter,' Ella added.

So, still hand in hand, brother and sister set off into the wood. Despite the fact that two suns shone down from above, the light dimmed as they made their way deeper among the trees. Shadows darkened, and the orange sky was all but hidden by the branches and creepers above them. Several times they stopped to listen, thinking they had heard something in the undergrowth, but, apart from a few birds, the wood was silent.

The day wore into evening and it became darker still.

There was no hint of civilisation. The twins had hoped that they might find a village or even a town, but the wood showed no sign of thinning or ending. *Perhaps*, they thought, *this whole planet is covered in trees and woodland.*

Through the covering of trees, twin moons shone down on the twin children. Asher and Ella had been walking for hours; they decided they must find somewhere to sleep.

'I suppose we shall have to sleep on the ground,' Ella said.

They found an area where the ground was slightly hollowed, and collected bracken and ferns to soften the hard floor of the forest. They kept larger branches and leaves to pull over themselves for warmth. They were both hungry, but they were even more tired; before long Asher and Ella were asleep, each clutching the other in a comforting embrace.

While they slept, the forest watched.

A pair of eyes glinted in the moonlight, staring out from among the trees. Soon, another pair of eyes joined it. Then more. Gradually, cautiously, the watching creatures emerged from the shadows and moved closer to the twins, curious about these strange creatures who had fallen from the sky. As the night grew darker and colder, the creatures spread more leaves over the sleeping children, to keep them warm.

When the morning sun struggled through the leaves and branches, Ella was the first to wake. Staring up at the roof of the forest, it took her several moments to remember where she was. She sat up slowly, blinking the sleep from her eyes. Then she saw the creatures gathered round, watching her and Asher. She grabbed her brother.

Asher was immediately awake, and pulled his sister to

him. Trembling, they both stared back at the strange animals
who were curiously watching them. The creatures were like
large dogs, but with elongated snouts and black-and-white
striped fur.

'I don't think they mean us any harm,' Asher said at last.
'They could have attacked us while we slept.'

One of the braver animals tentatively approached the
children. It was almost as big as they were. For a moment,
it stood looking closely at them, then it leaned forward . . .
and its tongue licked out across Ella's face.

Asher laughed at his sister's expression of surprise and
disgust. 'It just wants to be friends,' he said.

And so it did. Seeing the success of this first exchange,
the other animals also ventured closer. Asher and Ella patted
and stroked each of them; from the quiet mewing noises they
made – more like cats than dogs – they seemed to enjoy the
attention.

They obviously could not speak, but they understood
Ella when she asked them for food and mimed eating. The
animals led the way through the woods, and the twins found
themselves in an area where large yellow fruit hung from the
trees that grew out of the red grass. From somewhere nearby,
came the sound of running water.

Ella carefully took a bite from one of the fruit. She was
ready to spit it out if it tasted nasty or poisonous, but it was
sweet and delicious. The twins, who were starving, ate their
fill. When the children had finished eating, the animals led
them to a stream, where they scooped up handfuls of water
to drink. It was cold and fresh and tasted slightly sweet.

The animals looked after the children, showing them

where to find more fruit and water. They helped to drag
branches and logs from fallen trees so that Asher and Ella
could build a shelter. The obliteration module was too small
to be comfortable on its own, but they were able to strip out
the seats to make more space. The hatchway served as a
good door to the makeshift dwelling, and out the front of the
module they used the branches and logs to construct a kind
of porch. It was small and humble, but it was solid and kept
them dry and warm.

Neither of the children said it but they both knew that
they were destined to spend the rest of their lives in the wood.
While the animals were welcoming and helpful, and their
cottage – as they came to think of it – was comfortable,
every day followed the same routine: they ate, they explored
and they slept. Before long it started to grow repetitive, and it
made them miss their father and life they had lost all the more.

Then, one day, the man arrived.

He walked out of the trees and up to the cottage,
wearing a long cloak with the hood pulled up so that the
twins could not see his face. When he spoke, his voice seemed
familiar, but neither twin could quite place it – not then. He
had a large bag slung over his shoulder, which he set down by
the door when Asher and Ella came out to meet him.

'Happy birthday,' the man said.

The twins stared at him. They hadn't even realised that
it was their birthday.

'Who are you?' Asher asked at last. 'Where have you
come from?'

'We thought we were the only people on this planet,'
Ella added.

Then man nodded, his face shrouded by his hood.
'My name is not important,' he said, 'although I have come
a long way to see you.'

'To see us?' Asher asked. 'But why?'

'To bring you presents,' the man replied. 'And to see that
you are safe and surviving.'

Despite their entreaties, the man would not come into
the cottage. He waited while Asher and Ella opened the bag
and took out the things he had brought them – there were
packets of their favourite foods from Levithia, cartons of
drink and books to read.

'Thank you,' Ella said as she looked through it all. 'But
I still don't understand why you are here. *How* are you here?'

'There are people on this planet,' the man said.
'Although you are a long way from them here.' He pointed
into the distance. 'If you walked for a month in that direction,
you might eventually reach Arcadia. And that way,' he turned
to point in the opposite direction, 'lies the Capitol beneath its
protective dome. But that is even more distant.'

'Which place are you from?' Ella asked.

'Neither,' the man told them. 'I am not from this world,
any more than you are.'

'Do you have a ship?' Asher asked. 'Can you take us
away from this place?'

'I have a ship,' the man admitted. 'And one day I shall take
you away – but not yet. For the moment, you are safest here –
alone and hidden away. The new emperor of Levithia, your
uncle, believes you are dead. That is what keeps you safe. But
one day . . .' He let the thought hang in the air between them
for a moment, then he turned and walked back into the woods.

'Shall we see you again?' Ella called after him.

The man stopped and turned round. 'Oh yes,' he said. 'But not for a while. I have much to do, but I promise you I will return.' He continued walking away from them and soon he was swallowed up by the trees.

The days turned to weeks which then turned to months, but the man did not return. Asher and Ella began to enjoy their time in the wood – although they both felt it could never really become their home. The creatures, however, were friendly and, as the seasons changed, led the twins to different sources of food; in return, the twins helped the animals if they were sick or injured. They all lived together in a happy harmony, and the twins settled into their new way of life.

Asher and Ella did not realise that a whole year passed before the man again appeared out of the woods. As before, he hid his features beneath a hooded cloak, and brought with him gifts of food and books. This time, though, he accepted the twins' invitation to come into their cottage – he declined any food or drink, however, and he never once lowered his hood.

'Why won't you let us see your face?' Ella asked him. She and her brother had speculated often about why the man might keep his face hidden. They thought perhaps he might have suffered some disfigurement or injury, and Ella said so now. He simply laughed at the suggestion.

'You will know one day,' he said. 'But until that day I don't want to get your hopes up. Perhaps next year.'

They asked him what he meant by this, but he would be drawn no further. Soon he bid them farewell, wished them a happy birthday and walked back into the woods.

Intrigued, they began counting the days. Would the mysterious man return on their next birthday? That would be the day they came of age, the day they would have assumed the throne of the Levithian Empire. It was incredible how completely their lives had changed in such a short time . . .

The children passed the next year in much the same fashion as they had the previous one. They had grown well and truly accustomed to their life on this planet by now, and what had seemed repetitive and boring during their first year here had ceased to worry them – it was nothing more than habit, and they barely noticed the time passing.

True to their guess, on the twins' next birthday the man did indeed appear once more – but this time he brought no gifts. He arrived at the cottage and, as soon as Ella and Asher came out to meet him, he threw back his hood, revealing his face. It was a face they remembered well.

'Rigel!' Ella exclaimed.

'But it was you who murdered our father,' Asher said.

Rigel shook his head sadly. 'I did not kill your father any more than you did,' he said. 'Indeed, I loved him almost as much. But I know who did kill him.'

It was a warm afternoon so, rather than go inside the makeshift cottage, Rigel and the twins walked together through the woods while they talked.

'It took me a long time to uncover the truth – although, to be honest, I suspected it from the beginning,' Rigel told the twins. 'My friends helped me to escape Levithia before your uncle could have me executed. I could only return to Levithia in disguise, so I had to work in secret.'

'So who did kill our father?' Ella asked.

'I spoke to his physician,' Rigel explained. 'He is a good man, and he too was keen to find out the truth. Of course we could only meet secretly, but he told me that your father had been poisoned and the sort of poison that was used. It was a rare concoction, but eventually I managed to track down the source. Your father was much loved, so I was fortunate to have help. Just a few months ago, I discovered the identity of the man who provided the poison.'

'And killed our father,' Asher said. His face was dark with grief and anger.

Rigel shook his head. 'No. This man did not know who the victim would be. He was horrified when I told him, and only too happy to identify the man who had bought the poison from him – although he was scared, he did provide a sworn statement. I have had to tread carefully, though,' Rigel went on, 'because the man who bought the poison and murdered your father was his own brother – your uncle, Lord Grath.'

Asher and Ella were both shocked by this news, but in truth neither of them was much surprised. They all walked on in silence for a while.

'There are some other things you need to know,' Rigel said at last. He sat down beside the twins on a fallen tree on the banks of a fast-flowing stream before he went on. 'Firstly, the council has pardoned you both. They know you did not kill your father.'

'How do they know that?' Asher asked.

'The emperor's physician was able to prove when the poison must have been administered. Your father was away from the palace at the time, and neither of you was anywhere near him. So the council issued a posthumous pardon – they believe, of course, that you are both dead, blown up in the obliteration module.'

'They don't know it went wrong?' Ella said.

Rigel pulled a leaf from a nearby plant, and twisted it round his finger. 'It didn't go wrong,' he said quietly. 'It was sabotaged.'

Ella and her brother looked at each other, then back at Rigel. 'By you?' Asher asked. 'Is that how you knew we were here?'

Rigel nodded. 'It was the best I could do. I reprogrammed the onboard computer to crash-land here rather than detonate the explosives.' He looked around. 'Of all the planets within range, this one seemed to offer the best chance of survival. And,' he added, 'the people here have no interest in getting involved in the affairs of others. They watch and they analyse, but they rarely interfere.'

'We've been happy here,' Ella agreed. 'Although we would rather be at home.'

Rigel stood up, dropping the twisted leaf. 'Then home is where we shall go.'

'Really?' Asher and Ella said together. Ever since Rigel had first told them – in his disguise as the hooded stranger – that he would take them away from this place, they had barely dared to hope that they might truly be able to return home to Levithia one day.

'Really,' Rigel replied firmly. 'I have a statement from the man who sold the poison to your uncle. This statement, along with other evidence I have collected, proves beyond a doubt that Lord Grath assassinated the emperor. Your uncle is a

cruel ruler, and not loved as your father was – the council
will welcome any excuse to depose him.'

'Then why haven't they already done it?' Ella asked.

'Because there is no one to take his place – or so the
council believes. But now you are both of age, and you have
been pardoned of any crime – rightfully, you are the rulers
of Levithia. When you return, the council will depose
Lord Grath and have him arrested. I have already arranged
for the captain of the Palace Guard to move quickly when
the time comes.'

'Then it's true,' Asher said quietly. 'We can go home.'

'Thank you,' Ella said, taking Rigel's hand. 'Thank you
so much.'

'Will you advise us, when we are emperor?' Asher asked.
'We may be of age, but neither of us knows how to rule
an empire.'

Rigel smiled. 'I shall be happy to do whatever I can to
make your rule long and filled with wisdom. But there are two
things you have to do yourselves before I can truly help you.'

'Tell us,' Ella said. 'What must we do?'

'Since you have been pardoned, when you return to the
palace, you both – as the rightful rulers – will immediately
assume your role as emperor. The council will support you,
and your uncle will be forced to step aside. Your first act as
emperor must be to command the captain of the Palace
Guard to arrest Lord Grath – this must be done before your
uncle can rally support or attempt to seize power by force.'

'And what is the second thing we must do?' Asher asked.

Rigel smiled. 'I am still sentenced to death, although I
swear to you I had nothing to do with your father's murder.

Before I can return to the palace and become your advisor, I would welcome an imperial pardon.'

Asher nodded. 'I'm sure we can arrange that.'

'Of course we can,' his sister said.

And so the new rulers of the Levithian Empire walked back through the wood with their newly appointed advisor. They collected what few belongings they had from the cottage that had been their home, and said goodbye to the animals that had befriended and helped them. Then they climbed aboard Rigel's small shuttle and headed back to the palace where they had grown up, and from which they would now rule their empire.

THE THREE LITTLE
SONTARANS

nce, long ago, when the Sontarans and the Rutan Host had only been at war for a few centuries and their conflict was still young, there was a battle in the Klovian Cluster. The Sontarans drove their enemy back through the cluster, but the Rutans made a counter-attack and gained the upper hand – or rather the upper tentacle, for the Rutans are gelatinous, blobby creatures with tendrils and tentacles instead of hands or arms. The Sontarans were forced to retreat, their fleet in disarray and their battle plan in tatters. The Rutans, too, suffered heavy casualties. What had been a mighty battle across a vast area of space became fragmented; on planets across the cluster, Sontarans and Rutans faced one another in small groups, each side hoping to gain a strategic advantage.

On one of these planets, a Sontaran legion fiercely fought a Rutan battalion. They fought in the hills and the valleys, on the plains and in woodland, through deserts and in icy polar regions. The battle lasted for months, until there were just three Sontarans left alive, opposed by a single Rutan.

'We must establish defensive positions,' the first Sontaran said to the others. His name was Marshal Vrike and he was a veteran of several campaigns against the Rutans. 'We shall have the strategic advantage if we force the enemy to the offensive.'

'If we split up into separate fighting units,' the second Sontaran, Major Kyre, said, 'we shall stand a better chance of success.'

The third Sontaran, Commander Starn, agreed with Major Kyre. Out of all three Sontarans, and despite his relatively low rank, Starn had fought in the most battles. He had a deep scar down one side of his face that differentiated him from his otherwise identical comrades – it was an injury he had received off the rim of Landseer in the glorious retreat from Hastagart.

Humans had once colonised the planet the three Sontarans now found themselves on, although the humans had long since left. The decaying and abandoned remains of their time here still littered the planet, however, and the Sontarans had made their headquarters in the ruined shell of an old power plant that was built high into the side of a steep valley. The main structure was largely intact and the walls were strong.

From the power plant, the three Sontarans surveyed the landscape in front of them. They knew the surviving Rutan was located on the other side of the valley, and debated the route it might take to get to them. It would have to pass through an area of woodland.

'We should lay ambushes in the woodland,' Vrike

decided. 'Major Kyre and I will wait in hiding for the Rutan pest.' He turned to Starn. 'You may watch our inevitable and total victory from here. There is a good view down into the valley.'

If Starn was disappointed not to be involved in the ambush, he was disciplined enough not to show it. Instead he saluted, fist to chest, and said, 'I look forward to it, sir.'

As soon as the other two Sontarans had departed to set their trap, Starn set about securing the power plant. His superiors might be confident of victory, but Starn had survived thus far by planning for every eventuality, however unlikely. While the other two set their ambushes in the woods, Starn would make the power plant into a trap of his own, just in case . . .

Marshal Vrike took the forward position in the woods, as befitted his superior rank. He doubted that he would need the help of Major Kyre to destroy the enemy Rutan; he intended to finish the creature off himself, not just to enhance his own reputation but also for the greater glory of the Sontaran Empire.

'Sontar-ha!' Vrike chanted as he set about creating his ambush. He had decided that surprise was key so, rather than build a strong defensive position, he fashioned a camouflaged area where he could conceal himself and watch for the approaching Rutan. Vrike tore down leaves and branches, and wove a dense screen of foliage that he positioned between two sturdy trees. He ensured that there was a gap to see through, positioned so as to give him a good view of the woods ahead. When Vrike was satisfied that he could see but not be seen, he settled down behind his screen to wait.

As ever, one three-fingered hand was on his impulse blaster; the other never strayed far from the scissor grenade attached to his belt.

Vrike did not have to wait long. He soon saw the pale green glow that meant the Rutan was approaching. It was a tiny point of light at first, glimpsed through the trees, but it gradually grew brighter and larger as the creature approached. Vrike had only once fought a Rutan face-to-face – or, more fittingly, face-to-gelatinous-mass, given the Rutans have no head as such. As Vrike well knew, the Rutan's glow came from the electricity that filled its blobby green body. One touch from a Rutan's tentacle packed enough charge to kill – if it got close enough to touch you, that is. Vrike did not intend for the Rutan to get anywhere near him.

He aimed his blaster through the gap in the screen of foliage, and trained it on the approaching green glow. Not long now – he would just let it get a little closer and then he would discharge the blaster's entire power pack into the hated creature.

At that moment, the glow faded and vanished. Vrike frowned; he had been about to fire. Where had the Rutan gone? Surely it could not have just disappeared. He lowered his blaster, and peered more closely through the gap, looking from side to side and searching for any hint of the telltale green glow. But there was nothing.

Vrike's mind raced through the possibilities. The Rutan could not have retreated or he would have seen it. If it had changed direction, and started to head away from his ambush, then he should have seen that too. The only reason he could think of that he was no longer able to see the glow

was because it was hidden behind or beneath something.
The Rutan must be hiding.

In that case, Vrike decided, he merely had to wait for
the enemy to emerge from its cover. It made sense that the
Rutan was being cautious; it knew there were Sontarans in
the area, just as they knew that it was here. Vrike tried to put
his mind in the place of the Rutan, to think as it might think.
What would it do? What would he do in the same situation –
entering unknown and possibly dangerous territory where the
enemy might be concealed?

In his confidence of victory, Vrike had foolishly
overlooked one of the most basic tactics of the Rutans. The
Rutans were cold in every sense, coming as they did from an
icy world, but they knew the Sontarans were warm-blooded.
The Rutan might well have scanned for a heat trace, and, if
so, then it knew where Vrike was concealed. But that still did
not explain why the glow had disappeared. How could the
Rutan have possibly concealed itself?

Vrike looked around for inspiration. His deep-set eyes
settled on the dense undergrowth that grew close to the
ground. Could it be that simple? Had the Rutan ducked
down beneath the foliage? Was it even now forcing its way
through the undergrowth towards his position? Vrike let out
a snarl of rage and reached for his blaster – but he wasn't
quick enough.

To the side of Vrike, a whole area of vegetation was
suddenly uprooted and lit from beneath by an eerie green
glow as the Rutan burst from its hiding place. Vrike turned
to train the blaster on the creature but a long, pale green
tentacle had already snatched the gun from his grip.

Another wrapped suddenly round him. A massive charge of
electricity jolted through Vrike's armour and into his body.
Smoke poured out from the point where his helmet joined the
collar. His body convulsed, then fell lifeless to the ground.

Further up the valley, Major Kyre heard the sizzling
discharge of power. It was a sound he knew all too well, and
he knew what it meant. He paused in his work and took a
moment to pay silent tribute to his fallen comrade. But, even
in death, Vrike had given Kyre an advantage – Kyre now
knew where the Rutan was.

Kyre's own plan was more or less the same as Vrike's
had been. However, while the Marshal had concealed himself
behind a thin screen of vegetation, Kyre's defences were
altogether more robust. He had found a small clearing that
had been created by several large fallen trees. Whether this
was due to some weakness in the trees or the soil, or because
of a storm or some other natural event, Kyre neither knew
nor cared – it was the trees themselves he was interested in.

Using his osmic projector in cutting mode, he sliced
through the massive trunks and fashioned crude planks of
wood from the trees. These he lifted easily into position,
securing them with wedges cut from smaller fallen trees.
Before long, Kyre had fashioned a wooden stockade at the
edge of the clearing.

The disadvantage, he knew, was that the Rutan would
see where he was. The advantage, though, was in the strength
of his defences. He would let the Rutan reveal itself and then,
as his enemy wasted time, effort and resources assailing the
wooden walls, Kyre would launch his counter-attack.

Kyre had been positioning the planks that formed the

last of the walls when he heard Vrike's death. The Rutan was
not far away, but Kyre was almost ready. He lowered the final
planks into position from inside so that he was completely
enclosed within the stockade. In order to see out, he had
left small holes in each wall, and a section of one wall could
be swung away from the inside so that Kyre could emerge
to battle the Rutan when he deemed the right moment had
arrived. For now, he watched and he waited.

The planet's sun was starting to dip behind the ridge
where the old power plant was located. In the fading light,
the green glow of the approaching Rutan was even more
evident. Kyre watched it grow brighter and closer. *Soon*, he
thought with satisfaction, *battle will be joined*. He knew there
could be only one victor. Kyre would wait until the Rutan was
attacking the opposite wall – which he had made deliberately
weaker than the others so as to lure the Rutan to it – then he
would sneak out through the small door and circle round to
attack the creature from behind. His blaster fire would rip
through the inferior Rutan, and its green light would fade as
it died. Simple, but effective.

Except that in battle things rarely go exactly as planned.

The glow of the Rutan reached the edge of the clearing
and Kyre watched it move fluidly across the ground – half
rolling, half flowing – towards the stockade. Kyre could
have stepped out from cover then and shot at it, but he knew
from experience that it would take several sustained blasts to
destroy the Rutan. Also, it would be expecting an attack, and
be ready to loose one of its deadly tentacles. The moment
Kyre stepped out from his cover, he would be dead. No, it was
better to wait until he had the advantage of surprise, until the

Rutan believed it was in control and close to victory.

Kyre watched with eager anticipation as the Rutan approached the stockade. It inspected each of the walls in turn; there was a moment when Kyre thought it might have spotted the door, might try to prise it open, but the creature moved on. Soon it was back at the opposite wall, having concluded – as Kyre intended it would – that this was the weakest point and therefore the best place at which to make its incursion.

Kyre did not look out again to check what the Rutan was doing – there was a chance, if only slight, that it could weave a deadly tentacle through one of the peep holes. Instead, Kyre listened. He could hear the bubbling, hissing sound that all Rutans made. He could hear it squelching against the wall. There was something else as well – a grating, rubbing sound he could not identify. No matter. Whatever the Rutan was doing, its demise was fast approaching and inevitable.

Confident of victory, Kyre eased open the hidden door. He made his way quietly round the stockade, his blaster fully charged and levelled. When he reached the corner of the wall where the Rutan was working, he waited a moment, then leaped out, ready to blast the creature.

But there was nothing there. The Rutan was gone.

Kyre turned quickly, afraid it might have heard him coming, but there was no sign of the Rutan behind him or in the woodland nearby. He glanced upwards, checking it had not climbed to the top of the wall. Still nothing. Had Kyre looked down at the ground as well, he might have survived.

Instead, he retreated to the safety of his stockade to assess the situation. As soon as he had closed the door,

he stopped, silent and still. He could still hear the bubbling, hissing sound of the Rutan, as well as the unfamiliar scraping. Cautiously, he risked a look through the hole in the wall. But no, there was still no sign of the Rutan outside. In fact, Kyre realised, the sound seemed to be coming not from beyond the wall, but rather from somewhere lower down – as if the Rutan was underneath him.

Too late Kyre realised what the Rutan was doing. It had avoided the obvious strategy of coming *through* the wall; instead, it was coming *under* it.

Mud and soil exploded upwards as the whole floor of the stockade buckled and heaved. The walls were lit with a sudden green glow. Kyre managed to fire one bolt from his blaster before his whole body crackled with electricity and power surged through him. A moment later, the stockade walls exploded outwards in a massive electrical discharge.

Commander Starn saw the explosion from his position outside the power plant. He had also seen the smaller display of light when Marshal Vrike was killed earlier. His tongue licked out over his thin lips as he considered the situation. He had been prepared for the worst, and here it was. Starn was not worried, though – either he would be gloriously victorious or, like his comrades, he would die honourably in battle. Starn lowered his helmet over his head, sealed it in place, then turned and walked into the power plant, where he would fight the Rutan enemy.

The Rutan approached the power plant with caution. The thickness of the concrete walls meant that its heat sensors picked up nothing useful. It could not even be sure that the last of the Sontarans was inside the building, but it

seemed likely – if the Rutan itself was to set a trap, then the
derelict power plant was an obvious place.

The Rutan surveyed the structure, keeping well back.
It was aware that the glow it gave off was a disadvantage
unless it could be masked, so it made sure to stay behind
the trees and undergrowth, circling the building from a
distance. There were several entrances. All but one had been
completely blocked up, offering no chance of access, but the
last was not so secure. A heavy metal door was drawn across
it, but the metal at the top of one side was bent and corroded.
There was enough of a gap for the Rutan to tear back more
of the metal and create sufficient room to squeeze through.

Cautiously, watching for any hint of movement and
scanning for any point from which it might be observed, the
Rutan approached the damaged door. As it got closer, it could
see that the metal was shiny and not yet rusted where the
door was damaged. This could only mean that the damage
was new. Had the Sontaran damaged the door forcing it into
place? Or was there a more sinister reason for it – was this a
trap? The Rutan stopped to consider.

Inside the power plant Commander Starn waited in the
shadows, watching the point where he knew the Rutan would
have to enter the building. His blaster was fully charged,
and he had two scissor grenades remote-primed and ready.
He had heard the distinctive bubbling, hissing sound of the
Rutan as it approached the damaged doorway; Starn had
bent and torn the metal himself, making sure the damage
would be easily visible from outside. Now the sound faded.
The Rutan was moving away – but where was it going?

The Rutan slithered up the outside of the building.

The roof was the one area it had not been able to examine from the safety of the wood. It had a good understanding of how these primitive power plants operated, though, and had deduced that what it needed must be in this section of the roof.

Sure enough, the Rutan soon spotted a rectangular opening covered with wire mesh: a ventilation shaft. It calculated, from the angle of the shaft, that this would be ideal. The damaged door was obviously a trap – it was the only visible entry point, so the Rutan had to come in that way. But, while the Sontaran waited for the Rutan inside the damaged door, the creature would sneak into the power planet behind the Sontaran.

Congratulating itself on its superior strategy, the Rutan tore its way through the mesh grill and slithered into the shaft beyond. Taking care not to make any noise, the Rutan worked its way down the ventilation shaft. Before long it could see the light coming from the other end. The floor beneath the shaft's opening was covered in debris, but the Rutan felt no discomfort as it dropped down with a squelching sound. It turned slowly, assessing which route to take out of the chamber it now found itself in. Soon, the Rutan thought, it would attack the Sontaran from behind.

But it was wrong about that.

There was a movement in the shadows, and the third Sontaran stepped out into the light. He held a blaster in one hand, and some sort of remote-control device in the other.

'Prepare to die, Rutan!' Commander Starn said.

The Rutan was surprised, but not worried. It could withstand a sustained blast from the Sontaran's weapon and would still have long enough to destroy its enemy. The Sontaran was well within reach of its tentacles.

'I knew you would guess the damaged entrance was a trap,' Starn said. 'But you were wrong. *This* is the trap.'

'Your blaster cannot kill me,' the Rutan retorted. It drew back a tentacle, ready to strike.

The Sontaran gave a throaty laugh. 'I know,' he said. 'But I don't need it.' Then he raised the device he held in his other hand and pressed the button on it.

As well as knowing that the Rutan would guess the doorway was a trap and look for another way in, Starn also knew that there was only one other way into the power plant – the ventilation shaft. The remote signal from Starn's device triggered the primed scissor grenades that he had positioned beneath the opening to the shaft and they detonated beneath the Rutan, blasting it to pieces. Blobs of green jelly spattered the floor and walls. The remains of the Rutan continued to glow for a few moments, then the light dimmed and died away.

Commander Starn surveyed the damage with satisfaction. He brushed a few splotches of gelatinous green goo from his uniform, holstered his blaster, then turned and marched away. Victory belonged to the Sontarans at last.

JAK ᴀɴᴅ ᴛʜᴇ
WORMHOLE

eroes can be found in the most unlikely of places. Perhaps we all have it within us to do great things, but may simply lack the circumstances or the reason to be heroic. For Jak, his journey to becoming a hero all started with a humble cow.

It was the last cow that Jak and his mother owned. Long ago, when Jak's father was still alive, their family farm had been successful and prosperous; they had owned a whole herd of the very best cows in the land. But things change. Disease had killed most of the cows, and Jak and his mother had been forced to sell the rest, along with the fields and pastures where the cows had grazed, in order to make ends meet. Now they had to face up to the fact that they had no other choice but to sell their very last cow.

She was a good cow – healthy and robust – and she would bring a good price at the market. But Jak knew that once the money from this cow was all used up there would be no more. Not unless they sold the farmhouse itself, and then where would they live?

So it was with a heavy heart that Jak said goodbye to his
mother and began the trip into the town, leading the cow
behind him and talking to it all the way to keep his spirits up.
As they neared the outskirts of the town, the houses gradually
became larger and grander. On their way past an especially
large and grand house, Jak heard a voice calling out from
behind the ornate metal gates. It was weak and faint, but the
words were clear: 'Help me, please!'

Jak looked around to see if there was anybody else about.
But he was alone – there was no one else the voice could
be calling to. So Jak went to the gates, and leaned forward
to peer through them. As he did so, one of the gates swung
slowly open. Curiously but cautiously, Jak went through.

A man was lying inside the gates, just out of sight of
the road. He was breathing heavily, and there was blood on
his shirt. Leaving the cow to graze on a rather fine stretch
of lawn, Jak ran to help the man. As he approached, he was
surprised to recognise him: it was Councillor Jevan, one of
the more senior of the country's officials.

'Councillor!' Jak gasped as he reached him. 'What
happened to you? I must get help.'

Councillor Jevan grabbed Jak's arm. He shook his head
weakly, and a trickle of blood ran out of the side of his
mouth. 'No,' he said quietly. 'It is too late for me. But I have
to make amends.'

'Amends?' Jak said. 'What for?'

'For what I have done. I have betrayed everyone.'
His breathing was laboured, and the blood bubbled at his
lips. Jak could see the councillor was not long for this world.

He listened as the dying man went on. 'Not through choice, you understand. I thought I was creating a bright future for our world. Riches and abundance. But I was tricked. And now, unless you help me, it is too late.'

'Too late for what?' Jak asked.

'Too late for us all.' The councillor's eyes widened. 'Tell me you will help,' he demanded.

'Of course – if I can,' Jak replied.

The councillor fumbled in his pocket, and finally managed to pull out a small metal object that was rounded like an egg and set with an intricate pattern of wires and studs. He pressed it into Jak's hand.

'What is this?' Jak asked. He had never seen anything like it before.

'I took it from the monster,' Councillor Jevan said. He was finding it difficult to speak. 'The monster I brought here.'

Jak looked around, horrified. But the councillor said quickly, 'It's all right. The monster is dead. I killed it.' He gave a rasping, throaty laugh. 'Though I fear it has also killed me.'

'But this –' Jak held up the metal object – 'what must I do with it?'

'Destroy it,' Councillor Jevan said. 'Destroy it before more of the monsters come. Destroy it quickly.'

Jak inspected the device. 'I have to get to market first,' he said. 'I have to sell the cow or we shall have no money.'

The dying man beside him convulsed with sudden laughter. 'Money? Here.' He pulled something else from his pocket. It was a cloth bag that jingled and clinked, and he pushed it towards Jak. 'Take this. Then go home and destroy that device.'

Jak took the bag. He eased open the drawstrings that held it shut, and peered inside. Aghast, he looked back at the councillor. 'But there's more money in here than I have ever seen before,' he said. 'I can't take this.'

He made to give it back to the councillor, but the man just stared back at him, not moving, not answering. It took Jak a moment to realise that he was dead. Jak stood there, unsure of what to do, and whether or not to take the man's money. There was no question that he and his mother needed it, and Councillor Jevan had no use for it any more.

Jak led the cow out of the gates, and set off for home. In his pocket, the bag of money jangled against the strange metal device.

When he reached home, Jak took the cow back to the one field they had left, which was behind the house. He found his mother, and told her what had happened. She listened and nodded, then told him he had done the right thing and that he must now destroy the device – he had been paid to do a job, and the job must be done.

Jak had no idea how to go about destroying the strange metal object. After some thought, he set it on the chopping block and swung the axe at it. But unlike the logs which split easily under the heavy, sharp blade of the axe, the device was not even dented. He put it in the fire, but the surface was not so much as charred, and when a log gave way and the device rolled out on to the hearth Jak found it was barely warm. He hammered it into the stone floor of the kitchen until his hands were sore and the stone was cracked, but the strange device wasn't even scratched.

As the sun dipped low over the distant hills and evening

turned to night, Jak took a spade from the barn and went out into the field behind the house. In the failing light, he dug a hole as deep as he could. Then he dropped the metal device into the hole, and filled the hole over again with earth. He had not managed to destroy the device, but he did not imagine it would do any harm buried so deep in the ground and he was sure that the monsters Councillor Jevan had mentioned would never find it there. Satisfied that he had done the best he could, Jak put away the spade and made his way upstairs to bed.

The next morning, Jak woke early. The sunlight was shining through his bedroom window the way it always did – except that this morning there was something different about it. It did not seem as bright as it should. Thinking it was perhaps a particularly cloudy day, Jak went to look out of the window. He stared in disbelief at the scene outside.

In the air above the field was a swirling mass of . . . nothing. Right above where Jak had buried the metal device, the air seemed to pour into an inky black hole, like water draining out of a sink. Jak pulled on his clothes and hurried outside for a closer look.

From where he stood on the ground in front of the swirling blackness, Jak could see that the hole extended backwards like a tunnel through the air. The darkness reached back and upwards, disappearing into the sky. *But if it is a tunnel*, Jak thought, *where could it lead?* There was only one way to find out. He walked slowly forwards, stretched out his hand and touched the blackness. It had no feeling at all. Slightly reassured by this, but still apprehensive, Jak stepped into the darkness.

Immediately all light vanished. Jak could see nothing. He took one step forwards, then another, but still he could see nothing. Jak was beginning to wonder whether it would be better to turn back, when the darkness in front of him seemed to tear apart, ripped away like a torn piece of paper. Jak stepped forward yet again and into another world.

He found himself standing in a wide corridor. Behind him, the air was a churning mass of darkness, just like the other end of the tunnel had been. Ahead, the corridor turned abruptly. Jak made his way cautiously along the corridor and found that it split in two, and one branch led to a large window. Jak glanced around to check there was no one about, then hurried over to see where he was – perhaps he would spot some landmark he knew. But when he looked out of the window he recognised nothing. He was looking out at the ruins of a city. The sky was filled with smoke, and debris covered the ground. Some of the buildings were on fire. Only the building he was in remained intact.

Jak's mind was in a whirl. Part of him was desperate to get back to the black tunnel and hope that it would take him home, but another part wanted to explore this strange, ruined world and find out what had happened here. He walked slowly back to where the corridors met. *Just a quick look*, he decided – he would walk a little way along the other corridor to see where it went. Then, back to the tunnel and home.

As he followed it, the corridor curved slightly. Jak passed several doors, but they were all locked. Other passages led off it, but Jak stayed in the main corridor. The last thing he wanted was to get lost in a labyrinth of passageways.

Jak had been walking for about five minutes when he

heard someone coming towards him. His first instinct was to hide – he was not supposed to be here and, judging by the view he had seen from the window, this was not a safe world to be in. He ducked into the shadowy entrance of another passageway and pressed himself against the wall. He could hear heavy breathing as whoever was coming got closer, then deep, growling voices. Two people talking. He risked a quick look out into the corridor.

They weren't people.

A short distance away, two creatures stood having a conversation. One of them had its back to Jak, but he could see the other clearly. It was the height of a tall man, and standing on two legs, but it had the head of a bull – complete with two long horns. Jak retreated into the darkness, straining to make out what the creatures were saying.

'You are sure the device activated?' one of them asked.

'The modulation signal is clear,' the other replied. 'But the wormhole has not appeared in the appointed place.'

'Then someone has moved the device. Perhaps Jevan betrayed us.'

Jak felt cold at the sound of Councillor Jevan's name. Were the creatures talking about the device that Jak had buried?

'Perhaps. But soon he will die. Everyone on his pathetic world will die when the Nimon continue the great journey of life.'

The creatures were moving again. Jak shut his eyes tight, hoping against hope that they would not come down the passageway where he was hiding. They passed by the end of it and kept walking.

'Is the princess secure?' one creature asked as they went by.

'Yes, I have just come from her. But she is of no use to us now. She can stay in this world and die with it, or be executed,' the other creature replied.

The creatures' voices faded into the distance. Jak stepped out from where he was hiding. The creatures were now between him and the swirling blackness of the tunnel – his only escape. He considered following them, but his curiosity was heightened by what he had heard, so he set off in the opposite direction, the way the creatures had come.

Jak was, when all was said and done, more than a little intrigued by the mention of a princess. Based on the fact that one of the bull creatures had said it had just come from the princess, Jak reasoned that she must be held captive somewhere along this corridor. As he turned a corner, he saw ahead of him a wide set of double doors. Outside stood one of the bull-headed creatures. The doors were held shut with a metal bar across them, and a single window in one door was covered with a grille. This could only be a prison cell.

Jak stepped back round the corner before the creature saw him. He was pondering what to do when he heard the heavy footsteps of another of the beasts approaching. He risked peering round the corner, and saw another creature stride up to the one guarding the doors.

'It has been decided,' the newly arrived creature announced as it reached the door. 'The princess is to be executed. See to it.' Without waiting for a reply, it walked quickly on.

Horrified, Jak continued to watch. The princess was

about to be killed, while he just stood here. But what could he do? He had to do *something*. There was only the one creature again now. It turned to the door and lifted the metal bar out of its sockets. It put the bar down to one side of the door, then pushed the doors open and strode into the room beyond.

Without pausing to think, Jak seized his opportunity. He ran quickly but quietly down the corridor and grabbed the metal bar. It was heavier than it looked, but he managed to heft it up on to his shoulder. Then he followed the bull-headed creature into the room.

Having worked on the farm all his life, Jak was quite strong, but seeing the hideous creature bearing down on the defenceless young woman who was held captive gave him extra strength. He swung the metal bar as if he was bringing his axe down on a log and hammered it into the back of the creature's head.

A snarl of pain escaped from the creature as it fell. Jak stood over it, ready to bring the bar down again, but the creature gave a groan and lay still. When Jak was sure it wasn't going to get up again any time soon, he turned his attention to the woman. Now that he had a chance to look at her properly, he saw that she was about the same age as he was. Her dress was stained and torn, and her face – which would otherwise have been rather pretty – was streaked with dirt and grime.

'You don't look much like a princess,' Jak said.

'You don't look much like a hero,' she retorted. 'But I think you just saved my life.'

Jak looked down at the fallen creature. 'Yes, I think I did.' He put the metal bar down and held his hand out in greeting. 'My name's Jak.'

'Jahanna,' she replied. 'And I *am* a princess – or I was before the Nimon arrived.' Jak realised that this must be what the bull-headed creatures were called – Nimon.

'We should get away from here before another one comes,' he said to the princess.

Jahanna looked at him sadly. 'And go where? These monsters have destroyed the whole world. There is nowhere to go. You saved my life for now, but I'm afraid we shall both soon be dead.'

Jak grabbed her hand and pulled her towards the door. It was probably not the way one should treat a princess, but he didn't worry about that. 'There is a way to escape,' he told her. 'And another world to save.'

There was no time for further explanations and, since he had just saved her life, Jahanna trusted Jak. She kept a tight hold of his hand, and together they ran from her cell. They paused for a moment to close the doors, and Jak slotted the metal bar back into place. Jak then led the way back down the wide main corridor. He hoped that the Nimon who had passed him earlier had taken a different return route; whether they had or not, he was sure they only had a little time before the princess's escape was eventually discovered.

Their luck held until they were almost back where Jak had first arrived. They had just reached the point where the corridor split in two when there was a furious roar from close behind them. Jahanna gave a shriek of surprise. Jak turned to look back, and saw that a huge Nimon was charging down the corridor towards them, its head down. The horns on the creature's head glowed a livid orange. A ray of fiery light shone from them, and the floor between Jak and Jahanna exploded.

Jahanna ran, with Jak close behind her. Too late, Jak realised that Jahanna had taken the wrong turn: ahead of them was the wide window that looked out on to the ruins of Jahanna's world. They were trapped.

Thinking quickly, Jak pulled off his jacket. He held it out, making it as large as possible in the hope of hiding the view of the window behind him and Jahanna. The Nimon roared once more, and came charging down the short stretch of corridor, apparently intent on impaling Jak on its horns. Its horns glowed again. At the last moment, Jak pulled his jacket aside, and leaped at Jahanna. He wrapped his arms round her and dragged her to the floor.

At the same instant, the Nimon's horns shot fire. The light passed over Jak and Jahanna, and hit the window behind them, which exploded into fragments of glass that showered down. The confused Nimon skidded and stumbled as it tried to stop its charge. Jak hoped it would carry on and disappear out of the broken window, but it came to a lurching halt right on the brink. Slowly it turned towards Jak and Jahanna.

Jahanna leaped to her feet. She ran at the Nimon, knocking into it hard with her shoulder. The creature stumbled backwards and teetered for a moment on the edge of the window. Then, with a bellow of rage and fear, it fell backwards. Jak grabbed Jahanna to stop her from toppling after the Nimon. They stood there together, catching their breath while looking below them to where the Nimon had fallen.

The swirling blackness of the wormhole still filled

the corridor. Jak took Jahanna's hand and assured her that
it would be all right, although he was far from certain it
would be. Her forehead was creased as she looked towards
the darkness. She seemed to be considering whether she
would be able to step into it and leave her world – however
damaged it might be – behind forever. But then two Nimon
appeared at the end of the corridor behind them, and
there was no more time to consider. Hand in hand, Jak and
Jahanna ran into the darkness. They tumbled out of the
wormhole, and landed in the field behind Jak's house in a
tangle of arms and legs.

'Those Nimon will be right behind us,' Jahanna gasped.
'And now that they know where the wormhole is all the
others will follow. They want to destroy your world, like they
destroyed mine.'

She looked around desperately. 'Why is it here? What
created the wormhole?'

'There was a device made of metal,' Jak said. 'I was told
to destroy it but I couldn't. So I buried it here.'

From somewhere deep inside the whirlpool of blackness
came a bellowing roar.

'We have to get the device,' Jahanna said. 'Before the
Nimon get here.'

Desperately they scrabbled at the ground beneath the
wormhole. It was soft from being dug the previous day, and
they scooped out great handfuls. Soon, covered in mud and
dirt, they saw the gleam of metal. In the blackness of the
wormhole above them, a shape was beginning to form.

Jahanna grabbed the metal object from Jak. 'It's a
black-light generator,' she murmured. Quickly she pressed

several of the studs set into the metal casing, and the device clicked open. Then she dropped it to the floor, and stamped down hard on the innards, grinding them with her heel.

A huge, dark hand reached out of the wormhole, grabbing at Jak – then suddenly it was gone. There was a terrible screeching sound, a roar of pain, and the blackness of the wormhole abruptly vanished. Jak and Jahanna stared in silent relief at the empty air. On the other side of the field, Jak's cow munched contentedly on the grass, as if nothing had happened.

Inside the house, Jak's mother also seemed to have noticed nothing. She had been counting the money that Councillor Jevan had given Jak; there was, she told Jak, more than enough to keep the farm running for years. More than enough for them to offer Jahanna a home. If Jak's mother wondered where the girl had come from, she did not ask. She took her son's word for it that she was homeless and needed their help and kindness.

Jak showed Jahanna the room that would be hers. He told her how sorry he was about her world, but how grateful he was that she had saved his.

Jahanna gave Jak a small, sad smile. 'I'm glad we are both safe now,' she said. She thanked him for rescuing her from the cell she had been kept prisoner in. Although she was filled with sorrow at the loss of her own world, she was relieved to be free of the constant fear she had felt around the Nimon.

After a sleep and a bath, Jahanna put on a dress that Jak's mother had kept since she was Jahanna's age. When Jahanna came down to join Jak and his mother for supper, she asked them, 'How do I look?'

Jak looked at the young woman with whom he had escaped. 'Like a princess,' he told her.

SNOW WHITE
AND THE SEVEN KEYS
TO DOOMSDAY

ong ago, in a cosmos far away, death came to Winter. The planet of Winter had been at peace for thousands of years, and its people lived together in harmony, from the tall aristocrats to the diminutive minesmen. They lacked for nothing and felt that they had everything, so they were unprepared and ill-equipped to oppose the tyrant who rose from within them.

There had always been kings, queens, lords and aristocrats in Winter, but for the most part the planet's rulers wanted what was best for the people; the general good, the preservation of peace and the well-being of the people of Winter were their main concerns. Sadly, all that changed when King Drextor came to the throne.

Drextor was the son of King Matthias, a great and noble ruler who had been loved by all. Drextor was of quite a different character to his father, however. From his earliest years, he craved power. He delighted in ordering people about, and went to great pains to see that he got whatever he wanted – the great pains being those he inflicted on others.

As a king, Drextor was not loved like his father. In the past, on the rare occasions when a ruler of Winter had overstepped the boundaries of their power, or begun to view themselves as more important than the people they served, that ruler was deposed. The aristocrats and the commoners would agree between themselves that the ruler must go, and a delegation of the aristocracy would simply inform the monarch that they were no longer the ruler of the people of Winter.

But King Drextor had taken precautions; he had made sure that this would not happen to him. Before he even came to power, Drextor had begun work on a machine, with the help of his father's artificers, that he was certain would allow him to rule unopposed and in whatever way he wanted. The machine was completed on the day of his coronation, and his first act as the new ruler of Winter was to show it to the council that advised the king on all matters. As the members of his council listened in horror, King Drextor explained how his Doomsday Machine could make the air itself burn. It could only be switched on by inserting seven keys into the seven locks, all of which the King kept safely stored in secret locations around his palace. Any opposition to his rule, the King explained, any attempt to remove him from power, and he would use the Doomsday Machine to destroy the whole of Winter.

The rule of King Drextor would have been long and cruel, except for two things: love and poison. Drextor was immune to neither. The woman he loved did not love him, but she pretended that she did in order to take the Doomsday Machine from the tyrant king. He was so blinded by his love for her that he did not even notice. He was likewise oblivious when she stealthily slipped deadly poison into his wine. Only when he was clutching at his burning throat did he become aware of the deception, but by then it was too late for him. His treasonous lover watched with satisfaction as he died.

With Drextor dead, it was up to the council to appoint a new ruler, but before they did there was the matter of the Doomsday Machine. The council decided that it should be displayed in the royal palace, as a reminder of Drextor's cruel tyranny and as a warning against the same thing ever happening again. To ensure the machine could never be used, and that doomsday would never come to Winter, the seven keys were taken and hidden. One key was hidden in each of the seven provinces of the land, and the people of Winter continued with their lives, happy and safe from tyranny.

Until Queen Salima came to the throne.

Salima was not the kindest ruler that Winter had ever had, but nor was she the cruellest. The council had occasion to rebuke her, but she always seemed willing to accept their criticism. She would hang her head, as if ashamed, and promise to make an effort to think of the people in the future. Outwardly, she had the appearance of someone making an effort to become a kinder and more generous person. The truth, however, was very different.

Malpeth White had worked at the palace all his life. When he was a junior groundsman, he fell in love with a kitchen maid named Elsa. By the time they were married and their first child was born, he was head gardener and his wife was the palace housekeeper. When they saw their baby daughter for the first time, Malpeth and Elsa thought her skin was as pale and smooth, as unblemished and beautiful as the palace lawns after a fresh fall of snow. So they named the child Snow White.

As she grew older, Snow White also began to work in the palace. She cleaned and she tidied, and she helped in the kitchens and in the gardens. All the while, she grew more beautiful, her skin retaining the perfect, soft quality for which she had been given her name.

One day, when Salima had been queen for over a year, Snow White was cleaning the room where the Doomsday Machine was kept on display. By this time, everyone in Winter who wanted to had seen it, and visitors were few and far between, so the room where it was kept was rarely cleaned. Therefore, as she crawled beneath the machine with her cleaning cloths, polish, dustpan and brush, Snow White was confident that she was alone. She worked with such focus and concentration that it was only when she saw two pairs of feet pass by, close to where she was lying, that she realised she was not alone at all.

Snow White paused in her work, wondering what she should do. There were two people, and they were talking in low voices, one of which she recognised – it was the queen. *If I reveal myself now,* Snow White thought, *it will seem as though I've been eavesdropping.* What's more, she had no idea how long the queen and the man she was with had been there. So, out of embarrassment rather than guile, Snow White stayed where she was, hidden from sight.

However, now that she knew the queen and the man were there, Snow White could not help but listen in to what they were saying. Much of it she did not understand, but it was clear that the man was an engineer. He explained to the queen how the Doomsday Machine was designed to work, and showed her the places where the seven keys had been removed. It was only as they discussed the keys that Snow White began to understand the purpose of their visit.

'If these keys are hidden away,' Queen Salima said, 'then what use is the machine to me? Unless you can make it work again, I shall forever remain at the beck and call of those fools on the council. I shall be cursed forever to do what the people believe is right and good.'

There was suppressed anger in her tone. The queen's voice had risen, and Snow White had no doubt at all that she had made the right decision in remaining hidden.

'It is my destiny to rule, to be obeyed, to have people do my bidding,' Queen Salima continued. 'Make this machine work again, and I shall truly be queen of Winter. The people will tremble when they so much as breathe my name.'

On one wall of the room was a large mirror. It had originally been placed there to throw more light on to the machine so that visitors could see it better; now, Snow White found that she could see the queen and the engineer reflected in it as they examined the machine. The engineer slid open a panel in the side of the machine, revealing a hidden screen.

'I have made an extensive study of the original plans of this device,' the engineer said, 'and you are right, of course, Your Majesty – without the missing seven keys it cannot

work. Nor is it possible to recreate these keys. But there is
a facility that the council do not know of which will help you
to gain the power you seek.'

Snow White strained to hear, and silently pulled herself
a little closer to the edge of the machine so as to get a better
view. The engineer was working at some controls, which
were set into a panel at the side of the screen.

'I do not pretend to understand exactly how this works,
or all that the device can do,' he was saying, 'but the machine
was designed to be a whole. It communicates with itself, not
just through gears and wires, but also through the air.'

A picture started to form on the screen. It was indistinct,
gloomy and dark.

'What use is that to me?' the queen demanded. 'And
why do you show me nothing but a darkened room?'

'But, Your Majesty,' the engineer said, his voice low and
husky with excitement, 'the machine *knows*.'

'Knows? What do you mean it knows?' the queen
snapped. Snow White could hear in Salima's tone that she
was quickly growing impatient.

'It knows where its missing keys have been hidden.
It can sense them. It can feel them. And, on this screen, it
can show us where they are.' Snow White could see the
engineer wringing his hands in the mirror. He looked just
as nervous as she felt.

All was silent while the engineer waited anxiously for
the queen's response. She looked at him fiercely for a
moment or two – then she laughed. The engineer appeared
to relax a little.

'The council does not know of this?' she asked at last,

when she had stopped laughing.

'No one knows of this, excepting myself and Your Majesty,' replied the engineer.

'And where is this room in which the first key is hidden?' the queen demanded.

The engineer looked down at the ground. 'Alas, that I do not know – all I am sure of is that this key is hidden in the province of Seazalon. But if we examine the image there will be clues. Find that room, and you shall find the key. It may be a long task,' he added, 'but if Your Majesty truly wishes to restore this machine to working order . . .'

The queen considered this. 'Show me the other keys,' she said at last.

The engineer pressed a button at the edge of the screen, and one by one the location of each of the other keys was shown. One was between books on a dusty shelf, another was resting on a high ledge above a window and was bathed in bright sunlight. One was under a rock beside a pond, another in the hollow trunk of an old tree beside a wide lawn. One was in a cupboard, hidden among all manner of bits and pieces, and the last key was hanging on a hook behind a large tapestry in a dining hall.

'I shall find them,' the queen said quietly. Even in the mirror, Snow White could see that her eyes were filled with burning ambition. In that moment, Snow White knew that she had to stop Queen Salima from acquiring the machine's keys.

The queen and the engineer talked for a while longer. Snow White paid close attention as the engineer showed the queen how to operate the screen, and listened carefully

as the queen made plans to try to work out where each of
the locations could be. By the time the two of them left,
Snow White was stiff from lying so still for so long, and her
throat was dry from breathing in dust. She pulled herself out
from beneath the Doomsday Machine, and wondered how
she was going to stop the queen.

She could, she thought, go to the council. But how
likely were they to listen to her? Would they take the word
of a young girl working in the palace over that of the queen
of Winter herself? It seemed unlikely – and, once Queen
Salima became aware that Snow White knew of her evil
intentions, the girl would not live long.

Being diligent, Snow White finished cleaning the room.
As she worked, she thought more about what she had seen
and heard; she wondered who she could tell, what she should
do. Her only course of action, she knew, was to try to locate
at least one of the seven keys to the machine before the
queen could.

This decided, and the room finally clean, Snow White
hurried over to the door and closed it – there was no way
of locking it, so she simply had to hope that no one would
come. Snow White went over to the machine, and opened
the panel in its side, just as she had seen the engineer do.
She struggled to remember which of the controls he had
used to activate the screen, but after some trial and error
the screen glowed into life.

Snow White stared at the dark image of the room where
the first key was concealed. There was little she could make
out that was of any use – the shutters were closed, and there
was hardly any light. From what the engineer had said,

Snow White knew that the key was in the centre of the image
– that meant it was inside a wooden trunk placed beside a
table that was piled high with books and papers. But Snow
White could not see anything which gave any clue as to where
the room she was looking at might actually be.

Reminding herself that she needed only to find one
of the keys, Snow White reached for the control she had
seen the engineer use and brought the next key up on the
screen. As she did so, though, she accidentally pressed
another button. She pulled her hand away quickly, afraid of
damaging something. For a moment, Snow White thought
that nothing had happened – but then she noticed that the
image seemed deeper and richer. It was now as though Snow
White was looking at the room through a window, rather
than seeing a picture of it on a screen.

Curious at the effect, she reached out and tapped the
screen . . . and her hand passed *through* it. Alarmed, she
pulled her hand back. She had felt nothing, though, and her
hand seemed fine, so she reached out once more. Yet again,
her hand went through the screen – in fact, her whole arm
did. It was as if she had reached right into the room. Snow
White withdrew her arm, trying to work out what
this meant.

She went and got a chair from the other side of the
room and placed it beside the machine. She then climbed up
on to the chair, so that she was high enough to lean forward
and push her head through the screen. Sure enough, she
found she was indeed *inside* the room. She looked around,
seeing parts of the room that had not been visible on the
screen.

When she turned to look behind her, she found
that, somewhat disconcertingly, her neck stopped at the
point where it came through the screen – if there had been
anyone else there in the room, they would have seen her
disembodied head staring at them.

Snow White withdrew her head, climbed down off
the chair and sat down to consider things. If she could get
into each of the rooms through the screen then she did not
need to know where they were; she could simply collect all
seven keys and bring them back through the screen to the
palace. There was just one problem: the screen was only
wide enough for Snow White's head to fit through it. There
was no way that she would be able to climb through.

But Snow White had an idea. Carefully, she slid the
panel back into place over the screen, being careful not to
touch any of the controls. She would leave the screen as a
window for now and return later, when everyone else in
the palace was fast asleep – and she would not be alone.

Among the people who worked for Snow White's father
in the grounds of the palace was a group of seven minesmen.
Their forefathers had worked in the mineral mines – their
shorter stature and leaner bodies meant they could squeeze
through gaps and into areas that no one else would ever
manage. Snow White knew the minesmen who worked for
her father well. They were friendly men, with long straggly
beards that reached almost to their feet.

So, as darkness fell, Snow White made her way to the
minesmen's hut in the palace grounds, where she knew
they would be about to have their supper of hot broth and
oatmeal bread. The minesmen listened attentively as she told

them what she had overheard and of the queen's plan. When she had finished her story, Elgar, the oldest and wisest of the minesmen, nodded grimly.

'We have each felt the queen's wrath,' he told Snow White. 'She is forever finding fault with our work, or ordering us about in the rudest manner. I thought it was because we were minesmen, but from what you say she would like to treat everyone with as much contempt.'

The other minesmen nodded their agreement. Snow White told them her plan.

While they waited for the night to grow old, the minesmen shared their broth and bread with Snow White. Then, once the palace was cloaked in darkness, Snow White led the minesmen quietly across the grounds to the palace. They snuck in through a small side door that she had left unlocked. When they reached the Doomsday Machine, Snow White opened the panel – she was relieved to see that the window into the other room was still open. The room was even darker now, for night had fallen across all the seven provinces of Winter.

Each of the minesmen was keen to help defeat Queen Salima's wicked plan. As the most senior, Elgar insisted on going first. He climbed up on to the chair, and disappeared head first through the screen. The others watched as he tumbled into the room beyond. He hurried over to the trunk, and retrieved the key that was hidden inside. Snow White reached her arms through the screen, and helped Elgar to scramble back up and through it.

Then Snow White moved the image to the next location. Each of the minesmen took their turn tumbling through the window and returning with one of the Doomsday Machine's keys. Finally, all seven of them had been retrieved.

'What do we do now?' Elgar asked.

'We destroy them,' Snow White said. 'Break them into pieces.' She placed six of the keys on the floor by her feet and held one in her hands, ready to try to snap it.

But, at exactly that moment, the door slammed open.

Queen Salima strode into the room. Her face was a grimace of rage as she stared at Snow White and the minesmen. Her eyes locked on the irreplaceable keys to her future power – laid out before Snow White, who held one in her grip, about to destroy it. The queen hurled herself at the girl.

But she wasn't fast enough. Snow White bent the key in her hands with all her might, breaking it in two. At the exact moment the key snapped, Snow White was knocked aside by the queen. So it was that when the key exploded in a glittering orange and red fireball it was not Snow White who was engulfed by the flames – it was Queen Salima.

The queen's screams echoed around the room. The other keys were caught in the blast and also exploded, one after another. Snow White huddled in the corner of the room, where she had been flung, sheltering her face from the flying debris with her arms. As the smoke cleared and the flames died down, she could see the crouched forms of the seven minesmen, who had taken refuge from the explosions in the other corners of the room and beneath the Doomsday Machine.

Snow White slowly got to her feet and the minesmen

ran over to her. She smiled down at the men who had helped her to save Winter once again from tyranny. Then, together, they turned to look down at Queen Salima, who now lay dead among the charred remains of the seven keys to doomsday, and her broken dreams of power.

LITTLE ROSE
RIDING HOOD

here was once a young girl called Rose who
lived with her mother near a deep, dark
wood. Rose's father had died when she was
a baby, and so her mother had brought her up on her own.
Rose was brave, fearless and clever, and every bit as beautiful
as the flower she had been named after. Her hair was like
spun gold and shone in the sunlight, and her smile brought
joy to all who saw it.

Rose loved her mother dearly, just as she did her
grandmother, who lived in a cottage on the other side of
the wood. Every week, Rose and her mother went to visit
her grandmother. Rose enjoyed these visits, and always
took some small gift for her grandmother, who would thank
her and, in return, give Rose something delicious to eat
and drink. Usually she would make tea, which was Rose's
favourite.

But one day Rose's mother fell ill. She wrapped herself
in a robe and lay down to rest. Rose looked after her mother

and cooked her meals. She even baked her some shortbread as a special treat.

The next day Rose's mother was much improved, but she was still not completely better. When Rose took her a cup of hot tea, her mother said, 'You know that today is the day we should visit your grandmother, but I'm too poorly to go out in the cold and walk all the way to her cottage.'

'Won't Grandma be worried if we don't visit?' Rose asked.

Her mother nodded sadly, taking a sip of her tea. 'I'm afraid she will.'

'Why don't I visit Grandma on my own?' Rose asked. 'I know the way, and I can take her some of the shortbread I baked for you yesterday.'

Rose's mother agreed that this was a good idea. 'But promise me,' she said, 'that you will not stray from the path on the way. The woods can be dangerous, especially for young people travelling alone. Stick to the path all the way to the clearing on the other side of the woods where Grandma lives.'

This was a promise that Rose was more than happy to make. She found the woods creepy and unsettling even when she was with her mother; she had no intention of leaving the path. Rose wrapped some shortbread in a cloth and placed it in the basket her mother always used to carry food and other purchases. Then she put on her boots, as the path was often damp and muddy, and because it was cold outside she wore her long red coat – with its wide scarlet hood, it was like a cloak, wrapping her warm and safe for the journey.

Rose kissed her mother goodbye and set off into the chill of the autumn morning. The sun was pale, filtered by the hazy clouds. When Rose entered the wood, the light faded even more and she found herself in a twilight world. Fortunately, for the first part of her journey, the path was wide and easy to follow. On either side, the trees stood tall and dark. Their leafless branches were like skeletal arms reaching towards the path, their twigs bony fingers twitching in the breeze.

But soon, as Rose made her way through the dimly lit woods, the path narrowed. In places it was barely wide enough for Rose and her mother to walk side by side when they came this way together. Rose had to peer into the shadows at her feet to make sure she was still on the path. Although she knew the route and had travelled this way a great many times, she felt nervous. She had heard the stories they told about the Bad Wolf – she had seen its name scrawled across walls and daubed on pavements in the town. She had seen 'Bad Wolf' written in the most unlikely of places, and here in the gathering gloom of the woods, she imagined the creature hiding behind every tree, ready to pounce.

So it was not at all surprising that, even though she was usually so brave and fearless, Rose cried out in alarm when a dark figure stepped on to the path in front of her. She had been staring down at the ground, being careful of where she stepped so as to make certain she did not stray from the path, when the figure appeared. She very nearly walked right into him.

As soon as she had cried out and lifted her hand to her mouth in horror, though, she realised that the figure was only a man – tall, slim and wearing a dark jacket. The man seemed as surprised as Rose was, but he smiled politely and stepped to one side. He did not, it seemed, worry about stepping off the path. Perhaps he did not know about the Bad Wolf.

'I'm sorry,' Rose said. 'You startled me.'

'No,' the man replied. 'I'm sorry. I should look where I'm going. Always putting my foot in it – in more ways than one.' He tilted his head slightly. 'I don't suppose you've seen –' he began, but then he stopped and smiled again. 'No, you wouldn't have done, or you'd have run off long ago.'

'Seen what?' Rose asked.

'Nothing. Doesn't matter. Don't let me keep you,' he said.

'Who are you?' Rose asked, pausing as she walked past him.

The man stared beyond her into the trees. 'I suppose I'm a sort of woodcutter,' he said. 'I cut out the dead wood and keep the forest healthy. I weed out the poisonous, strangling vines.'

Rose tried to remember what she knew about woodcutters. 'Do you have a shed?' she asked at last.

'Oh, yes.' The man's smile was now a wide grin. 'I have a shed. And you know what? It's fantastic.' He raised a hand and gave her a quick wave. 'Bye then.' He turned and walked quickly off into the shadows, never once looking back.

It seemed to Rose as she continued walking that the woods were closing in on her. The path got narrower, and the trees grew nearer to the path. The glimpses of the sky that she saw through the dense branches above became fewer and farther between. Perhaps it was her imagination, but Rose fancied she could hear something close behind her.

Not on the path, but nearby, in the trees; something that followed and watched her. The hairs on the back of her neck prickled beneath the red hood, which she had pulled up over her head.

She stopped suddenly several times, listening. Was that someone close by, or just the echoing trace of her own last footstep? She peered into the deepest shadows, but she did not dare to step off the path. Once, she was sure she caught a glimpse of something – a hunched, misshapen figure moving quickly out of sight behind the broad trunk of a large tree. But, although she watched carefully for a full minute, there was nothing – no movement, no figure, no sound. Nothing.

The further she went, the more certain Rose became that it was not her imagination playing tricks on her. There really was someone – or some*thing* – following close behind her. She called out, her voice trembling: 'Hello? Who's there? Is that you, woodcutter?'

But there was no reply – just the rustling of the branches in the cold, biting wind.

With relief, Rose recognised a sharp turn in the path ahead. She was not far from the clearing where her grandmother's cottage stood. Just a few more minutes and she would be safe inside, laughing with Grandma about how silly she had been to imagine all sorts of horrors in the woods. Her grandmother would tell her that she was fine and safe, and that there was no such thing as the Bad Wolf; that it was just a story people told to scare children.

Rose reached the sharp bend. And, from close behind her, there came the sound of a branch breaking as though someone had stood on it. Rose froze. Slowly, hardly daring to

move for fear of what she might discover, she turned her head
to see where the sound had come from. A dark shape rose
up from the ground beside the path. Rose caught a confused
glimpse of its hunched body, of skin gnarled like an old
tree and deep-set eyes gleaming in a face on a bulbous,
neckless head.

A glimpse, no more. Then Rose was running. Her
heart pounded in her chest at the same frantic beat as
her feet pounded on the path. She dared not look back;
she could only run. Before she knew it, she was among the
trees. Somehow she had left the path. Somehow she was
running through the thickest part of the woods, with no
idea which way to go. She skidded to a halt, turning in a
full circle, trying to get her bearings, desperate to find the
gap in the trees where the path must be. But there was no
sign of it. She was not even sure which way she had come.

Rose did the only thing she could: she kept running,
hoping that soon she would find the path again or her
grandmother's house on the edge of the woods. She stared
into the distance, hoping to find a spot where the light was
brighter and the trees thinned.

Finally, almost sobbing with relief, Rose saw light. She
ran towards it, stumbling as her foot caught on a tree root.
She was breathing so hard she couldn't hear if she was still
being followed. She expected a hand or claw or paw to slam
down on her shoulder at any moment and drag her back into
the darkness. But she reached the edge of the trees and saw
that she had arrived at the clearing where her grandmother's
cottage stood. The path snaked in from the other side, and
the light she had seen shone from one of the windows.

Rose half ran, half staggered to the front door. It was rarely locked – *although perhaps,* she thought, *it should be.*

Sure enough, the door opened easily and Rose practically fell inside. As soon as she had caught her breath she called for her grandmother. The old lady appeared at the end of the hall. She seemed less frail and bent than Rose remembered, but Rose was so relieved to see her that she thought nothing of it. A few minutes later Rose was sitting on an old, threadbare seat in the living room, and her grandmother sat nearby in her usual, equally threadbare armchair.

Once Rose had recovered and got her breath back, she explained that her mother was ill. She told her grandmother about her journey through the wood, and about how she had glimpsed the misshapen figure coming after her.

Grandma smiled thinly. Was it Rose's imagination, or were the old lady's teeth a little whiter and straighter than she remembered?

'I'm sure it's all in your imagination, dear,' her grandmother said, as if sensing Rose's thoughts. 'We see all sorts of things in the dark and shadows that turn out to not be there at all.'

Feeling better now that she was out of the woods and safe in the cottage, Rose offered to make tea. Unusually, instead of fussing around Rose and helping, Grandma stayed sitting in her chair. Rose put the shortbread she had brought with her out on a plate – she was glad she had not dropped the basket in her haste through the woods.

'Thank you, my dear,' Grandma said, as Rose set a cup of tea down on the small table beside her.

'Would you like some shortbread?' Rose asked. 'I made it myself.'

'Perhaps in a minute.' Grandma nodded slowly. Usually she drank her tea hot, as soon as it was ready, but today she let it stand and cool while Rose talked about all the things she had done in the last week.

'It sounds very exciting, my dear,' Grandma said when Rose was done. She still had not touched her tea.

It struck Rose as odd that her grandmother had not once called her by name. Grandma did seem different today: colder, a little harsher, less interested, not as talkative. And her teeth were definitely whiter – perhaps even sharper too. Rose excused herself, saying she wanted another cup of tea.

As she left the room, Rose looked back at her grandmother sitting in her favourite chair. She could see the old woman's reflection in a mirror on the other side of the room. For the briefest moment, as she glanced at the mirror, it seemed to Rose that the reflection was not that of an old woman but of a gnarled, hunched creature with deep-set eyes and no neck, covered in suckers. Just for an instant, then it was Grandma again. Perhaps the journey through the woods had unsettled Rose even more than she realised.

But then there was the noise. To get to the kitchen, Rose had to pass the door under the stairs that opened on to steps leading down into the cellar. It could have been the wind in the trees outside, or perhaps it was a door banging somewhere else in the house, but Rose was sure she could hear a low, bumping, thumping sound – and it seemed to be coming from the cellar.

Rose took her empty cup through to the kitchen, then

she tiptoed back to the cellar door. She pressed her ear against the rough wood and listened. There was definitely a sound coming from the cellar – a sort of pulsing humming. Slowly and carefully, Rose eased the door open. She froze as it creaked, and she glanced back towards the living room, but there was no sound from her grandmother.

The sound from the cellar was louder now that the door was open. Rose decided against closing the door behind her, fearing that it would creak again, and she stepped through and on to the first step. The cellar below was bathed in a warm red glow. Rose carefully made her way down the steep stone steps. She had only been in the cellar once before that she could remember, when Grandma had asked her to put a box of ornamental objects she no longer wanted to have out on display down there.

When she reached the bottom of the steps, Rose saw that the glow was coming from the far end of the cellar. Against the wall stood something rather like an upright cabinet – except that it looked as if it had not been made, but *grown*. The material it was made of was like gnarled, twisted wood only it was a deep orange rather than brown. Stepping closer, Rose saw that there was a figure standing inside the cabinet – a figure she recognised at once.

'Grandma?' she whispered.

Rose ran down the last few steps. Her first thought was that her grandmother was asleep; her eyes were closed, and what looked like tendrils of the strange orange material were attached to her head. Rose's second thought was that, if this was her grandmother, then who was sitting upstairs in the living room, ignoring their tea?

The sound of a footstep on the stairs made Rose turn round. And there, staring at her and bathed in the pale red light from the cabinet, was her grandmother – her *other* grandmother. But, even as Rose watched, the old woman's form began to blur and shimmer. Her outline became indistinct, her features running like a watercolour painting in the rain. Gradually, they reassembled into a different shape.

The hunched, misshapen figure that Rose had glimpsed in the woods now stood on the stairs watching her. Its skin was textured like the cabinet behind her, and its dark eyes stared out from a neckless head covered in suckers and nodules. The creature gave an angry hiss. 'So the body print did not deceive you,' it rasped.

The creature advanced down the stairs, and started across the cellar towards Rose. She felt suddenly calm, knowing that whatever happened she had to get away and find help. She waited until the grotesque creature was almost within touching distance. Then, as it reached out, suckers on the ends of its fingers trembling and constricting, Rose threw herself to the floor and rolled under its outstretched arm. She managed to get her feet back under her and was up and running.

At the top of the steps, Rose looked back. She hated to leave her grandmother alone and helpless in the cellar with the creature, but she had no choice. She shoved the door closed behind her and ran down the hallway. When Rose tore the front door open, a dark figure was standing there, staring back at her. It took her a moment to recognise the woodcutter she had met on her way to her grandmother's. Rose tried to stammer an explanation, but the woodcutter put his hands on her shoulders and moved her gently aside so he could come into the cottage. He stared past her at the creature, which was now emerging from the cellar door behind Rose.

'Zygon,' he exclaimed. 'I knew it!'

The creature gave another angry, rasping hiss. It stood, framed in the cellar doorway, as the woodcutter ran full pelt at it. His shoulder struck the creature right in the chest as it stepped into the hallway. For a moment, time seemed to stand still. Then the creature pitched slowly backwards. It let out a wailing roar as it disappeared through the cellar door. Rose heard it tumble down the steps. There was another quieter wail, and then silence.

The woodcutter had grabbed hold of the door frame to stop himself from falling through after the creature. He stood and stared down into the cellar for a moment, then he turned towards Rose. A smile appeared on his face as if it had been switched on suddenly. 'Stay here,' he said. 'Back in a tick.'

Rose stood in the hallway, arms folded across her chest and trembling as if she was cold. After what seemed an age, she heard the sound of footsteps on the stairs. Then Rose's grandmother – her real grandmother – stepped through the door. She looked old and pale and weak. But she smiled at Rose.

'That nice man says I could do with a cup of tea,' she said. 'And you know, Rose, I think he's right.'

They sat down, and this time Grandma drank her hot tea, just as she always did when Rose came to visit. Their conversation, however, was a little different from usual – they both spoke of what they had experienced that day and comforted one another. Grandma told Rose how frightened she had been by the creature, and Rose told Grandma about

her mother's illness, and described her journey through the
wood and her adventures in the cellar.

'Right, all sorted,' the woodcutter said as he joined them.
Rose had made him a cup of tea too, and he drank it in a
single gulp, not bothering to sit down. 'You shouldn't have
any more trouble with the Zygons, and I've dismantled the
body-print equipment. Thanks for the tea. I'd better be going
now. Bye.'

He didn't wait for Rose and her grandmother to thank
him, but strode from the room and out of the cottage.
Rose watched from the window as the woodcutter headed
towards a small blue hut close to the path. She remembered
that he'd told her he had a shed; and, as the woodcutter
went inside, she thought how funny it was that she had
never noticed it here, so close to her grandmother's cottage,
before. As she turned to ask her grandmother how long it
had been there, her words were drowned out by a sudden
scraping, wheezing sound. Dry leaves blew against the
window in a flurry. And, when they were gone, so was the
woodcutter's shed.

THE
GINGERBREAD
TRAP

nce, long ago and far away, there were two children called Malkus and Everlyne. They were brother and sister and, although they argued often and teased each other, they also loved one another very much. Malkus would do anything for his sister, and Everlyne would have died for her brother – although she never thought it would come to that.

The children often played in the forest that lay between the dwellings where they lived and a great lake. They always kept to the paths they knew and the areas they recognised. Their parents had warned them of the dangers that lurked in the shadows between the trees, and the children were careful to never step beyond familiar trails.

Whenever he couldn't sleep, Malkus loved to sit at his window and stare out at the night sky. He knew many of the stars and constellations by name, and their twinkling beauty entranced him. He would often wonder if there were other worlds like his own out there, circling those stars, and if there were people like him and Everlyne living on those worlds.

But one night when Malkus gazed out his window there
was an extra star – a bright star he had never seen before.
It appeared at the edge of the constellation called the Lion's
Paw and, as Malkus watched, grew steadily brighter and
larger. It was moving, he realised. He followed its progress
across the sky with fascination. The star continued to
grow brighter, and as it fell towards the world it became a
burning ball of fire, then streaked down until it disappeared
somewhere in the depths of the forest.

The next day at breakfast, Malkus told his family about
the falling star, but it seemed that he was the only one who
had seen it. When he described it, his mother smiled in the
way she did when she thought he was making up stories –
it was clear she had not seen the star and that she did not
believe Malkus had either. Perhaps she thought he had
dreamed about it.

Everlyne, however, was captivated by Malkus's story of
the star that had fallen from the sky. When their mother was
clearing their breakfast away and had her back turned to the
children, Malkus whispered to Everlyne that the two of them
should try to find where the star had landed. Everlyne,
delighted at the idea, immediately agreed.

And so they set off into the forest, heading in the
direction that Malkus was sure the star must be. It proved to
be a long walk. They passed by all the places where they and
the other children from their town usually played – the old
stumpy tree, the clearing full of fairy rings and the standing
stone with the iron ring in it. After what seemed an age, they
found themselves in the deepest and darkest part of the forest.

The day was growing old, and they had walked further into the forest than they ever had before.

'Maybe we should go back,' Everlyne said, and she looked around nervously. She was not happy to be so far from home, and she was tired and hungry. Malkus was relieved; he too was desperate for something to eat, but hadn't wanted to be the one to suggest they turn back. In truth, he was beginning to wonder if perhaps the falling star had been a dream after all. How could a star fall from the heavens?

They turned and walked back the way they had come – or so they hoped. They had left the path behind long ago and in the depths of the forest one tree looks very like another. It did not take them long to realise that they were lost. Everlyne sat down on the trunk of a fallen tree that neither of them recalled having seen before, and buried her face in her hands. She did not cry – she rarely cried – but Malkus could see that she was just as upset and worried as he was. He sat down beside his sister, put his arm round her shoulder and held her tight.

'It can't be long before we find a path we know,' he said gently. 'If we walk in a straight line, we must eventually get out of the forest. And if we are going the wrong way then we shall arrive at the great lake and we can walk home along the road.'

They walked for another hour. Sometimes they were sure they recognised trees and bushes, branches and undergrowth; other times they were certain they had never been this way before. At last they reached a clearing. The sun was very low in the sky by now, and it shone through the gaps in the forest. The clearing did not look natural to the children, though;

it seemed as if something had uprooted the trees, thrusting them aside as it burned its way through them, and leaving the ground where they had been a charred and blackened mess.

'What could have done this?' Malkus said.

'A star, perhaps?' his sister wondered.

Ahead of them, standing at the end of the burned path, they could see what looked like a little house. As they approached, they saw that it was a cottage – a cottage that appeared to be made of things that were good to eat. The walls were made of gingerbread, and the window frames were icing. The handle on the front door was a sugared jelly, and the whole house was studded with sweets and chocolate. The hungry children ran towards the house, desperate to break bits off and stuff them into their mouths.

'We should ask,' Everlyne said as they got closer.

Malkus agreed. But, when they knocked at the gingerbread door, there was no answer.

'Perhaps no one lives here,' Malkus said. 'And, if they do, I'm sure they won't mind if we break off just a little bit to eat.'

As he spoke, the door swung slowly open. Inside, the children could see a large dining table piled high with more food and sweets, puddings and cakes and biscuits. Without another word, they hurried inside . . . and the house vanished.

One moment they were running towards the table piled high with food, and the next they found themselves in a plain metal box. They stopped and looked at each other in disbelief. Metal bars slammed down behind them, closing the box. Malkus and Everlyne were trapped inside.

They turned and ran to the bars, but could not move them.

They hammered on the metal walls and shouted for help, but no one came. They sat on the cold, hard floor and stared out at the darkening forest. After what seemed an age, they saw a figure making its way slowly towards them. An old woman, hunched and wizened, walked slowly up to the metal box and peered through the bars. Her skin was wrinkled and grey, and her eyes were small and dark. Her nose was a crooked beak with a wart on one side, and her teeth when she smiled were yellowed and cracked.

'Can you help us get out of here?' Everlyne asked.

The old woman responded with a cackling laugh as brittle as old, dry leaves. 'Let you out?' she said. 'Why would I let you out when I've gone to so much trouble to get you in?' She stared at the children through her pinprick eyes. 'You look as if you need feeding up,' she said. 'If I bring you dinner, do you promise to eat it all with no fuss?'

Malkus and Everlyne, though scared, were both starving by now. They agreed to eat whatever the old woman brought them.

'So long as it's proper food,' Malkus said. The old woman looked so much like a witch that it would not have surprised him if she had brought them a plate of dead spiders and worms. Or worse.

But the children were pleasantly surprised when she returned a while later with two large bowls of hot fried potato slices. She told them to move to the back of the cage, then she pressed a switch that was on the outside wall and the bars slid away. The children could not see the switch from inside the cage, but they heard the click as it was pressed. The old woman left the bowls of fried potatoes on the floor of the cage,

then pressed the switch again and the bars moved back
into place.

Night fell, and the old woman passed two thin blankets
between the bars. The children curled up under them, cold
and afraid. The moon was a large, pale disc high above them,
visible through the bars of their cage. As Malkus dozed,
Everlyne stared up at the moon, and thought about the falling
star that had brought them here and how she should never
have agreed to go and look for it. But it was too late now;
what was done was done.

As she stared up at the moon, a shadow passed across it.
At first she thought it was a bird. Wings flapped against the
moonlight and the creature twisted and turned, and Everlyne
saw that it was a bat – but it was unlike any bat she had seen
before. Its shape was harder and more angular, and it was
huge. She heard the beat of the creature's wings, and saw its
shadow drop back towards the ground on the other side of
the cage. She listened, holding her breath, and fancied she
could hear it moving about beyond the metal wall. Then,
after a while, all was silent and she breathed again.

When the sun rose above the trees the next morning,
both children had barely slept. Everlyne told Malkus about
the enormous bat. Had she dreamed it, she wondered? Had
she dozed off for a few minutes and imagined it all?

The old woman brought them fried potatoes for each
meal throughout the day. The potatoes were good – the best
the children had ever tasted, although they were hardly in any
position to appreciate them.

On the third day, the old woman told the children
she needed their help. If they agreed to help her then

perhaps – *perhaps* – she might let them go free.

Malkus hoped this might offer them the chance to escape, to run off when the old woman was distracted. But it soon became clear that she would only let one of the children out of the cage at a time to help her – and neither Malkus nor Everlyne would leave the other behind alone. If one of them ran off, who knew what the old woman would do to whoever was left behind?

Malkus was the first to be allowed out. Everlyne watched, her face pressed to the bars, as the old woman led Malkus to where, not far from the cage and half buried in the ground, a long metal object lay. It was as big as a small house, and its sides were blackened and pitted. Malkus realised that this must be the object he had seen falling from the sky.

It occurred to Malkus just how easy it would be for him to overpower the old woman; he was young and healthy and strong, while she was old and weak and frail. He could then use the switch to open the cage and set Everlyne free, and they could both escape. But, as if she knew what he was thinking, the old woman put her hand on his shoulder. He was surprised at how strong and firm her grip was – and, when she squeezed, the sudden pain that shot through him made it obvious that the woman wasn't one bit as old or weak or frail as she appeared. She would not be the one who was overpowered in any fight.

The old woman opened a hatch in the side of the metal star, and shoved Malkus through it. Inside, the metal star was filled with screens and computers and the sort of advanced equipment that Malkus had only heard about. The old woman sat him in front of one of the screens and told him to start work.

'But I have no idea how to work this,' he told her, afraid
that once she learned he was no use to her she might kill
them both.

'You'll surprise yourself,' she said.

And he did.

Malkus had no idea how it was possible, but the images
and words that appeared on the screen in front of him
somehow made perfect sense, and he knew exactly what to
do in response to them. He looked at the woman in surprise,
and for the briefest moment it seemed as if she was not an old
woman at all but a huge bat with leathery wings spread out
behind her.

Then she was a hunched, witch-like woman again.
'It's amazing what a good diet can achieve,' she said.

She left Malkus to work, and walked stiffly away to the
other side of the metal star. When Malkus glanced over, he
saw that she was standing beside a small metal cabinet and
he watched as she lowered a wire basket of sliced potatoes
into it. At once the whole place was filled with sizzling and
the smell of cooking. The woman seemed wary, standing well
back from the fryer (for that was clearly what it was). Malkus
assumed she was afraid of being burned by splashes of the
hot oil. He could see large metal barrels stacked to one side
of the fryer, and guessed they were filled with the cooking oil.

The old woman left a bowl of fried potatoes for Malkus
to pick at as he worked, and took another bowl to Everlyne
in the cage.

Malkus worked at the screen until his eyes were heavy
with tiredness; then the old woman led him back to the cage,
and brought Everlyne out to take her brother's place.

Everlyne was also surprised by how she was able to work at the screen. Everlyne continued working where her brother had left off, and as she progressed she began to see the purpose of what they were doing – the metal star was broken, and she and Malkus were repairing it with their work at the screen. Once the work was done, the old woman would return to the stars and the children would be free.

Except Everlyne did not believe the woman would set them free. Perhaps it was the way she watched Everlyne hungrily when she thought that Everlyne was not looking. Perhaps it was Everlyne's growing understanding of the creature they were dealing with – for she was now certain that the old woman and the bat creature were one and the same being. Perhaps it was simply instinct that warned Everlyne that, when their work was done, the woman would kill the children as easily as she seemed to lift the heavy barrels of oil to refill the fryer.

Talking quietly that night, as they lay beneath their thin blankets inside the cage, both Malkus and Everlyne agreed that, as well as not being as weak as she appeared, the old woman was not an old woman at all.

'It's like how the house made of gingerbread turned out to actually be this cage,' Malkus said. 'She can make things look like something else – even herself.'

They talked long into the night, discussing how they might escape from the old woman who was not an old woman.

'It's the potatoes,' Malkus said. 'Or rather the oil she fries them in. That's what has made us clever enough to solve the problems on the screens and repair the metal star.'

'And it's also made us clever enough to escape,'

Everlyne said. 'Clever enough to wonder why she needs
us at all. If the oil and the potatoes have given us the ability
to mend the star, why didn't she just eat the potatoes and
get clever enough to make the repairs herself? Why bother
to set her gingerbread trap and hope someone would
come along?'

'Perhaps she can't eat the oil,' Malkus said. He told his
sister how he had noticed the old woman was wary of the
spitting hot oil. Everlyne told her brother how careful she
had seen the old woman was when pouring the oil from the
barrels into the fryer.

'She is scared of the oil,' Everlyne decided.

'And not just of eating it,' Malkus agreed. 'She has to
avoid even touching it.'

Together, huddled under their blankets on the cold, hard
metal floor of the cage, they made their plan.

The next morning, when the old woman took Malkus
to the metal star to begin his work, he asked if he could have
some fried potatoes before he started. 'I don't know why,' he
lied, 'but having just eaten makes me work faster and harder.'

The old woman nodded, as if this was understandable,
and made her way over to the fryer. Rather than sit at the
screen, as he usually did while she fried the potatoes, Malkus
followed her. As the old woman took her position in front
of the hot oil, Markus wandered over to the stack of barrels
and began unscrewing one, as if he was going to help the old
woman add more oil to the fryer.

'You are very unobservant,' the old woman said, walking
over to where Malkus stood. 'We will not need any more oil
for a while yet.'

'Oh, we will need it,' Malkus told her. 'For this!'

And as he spoke he threw himself at the old woman, shoving her in the shoulder with all his strength. The old woman let out a piercing shriek as she fell to the ground. A look of pure fury crossed her monstrous, ancient face.

But Malkus did not see this. As soon as he had barged into the woman, he grabbed the barrel next to him, fumbling frantically to finish unscrewing the cap. Malkus pushed the barrel over in the direction of the old woman and thick oil began to pour out of it.

Still sprawled on the ground, the old woman saw the pool of oil running rapidly across the floor towards her. She shrieked as the first trickle came into contact with her skin – where it touched her, the old woman's flesh steamed and sparked like damp logs on a winter fire.

Her shrieks became a high-pitched scream and, in an instant, the old woman was gone. There was a blur of movement and the huge bat appeared in her place. Its wings unfurled, beating at the air.

But it was too late. Before the bat could get off the ground, the oil had puddled over its gnarled, bony feet. The bat let out a final piercing shriek, and then the whole place was lit up in a sudden flare. Malkus ducked away as the creature exploded into smoke and flame. When he looked back, the bat creature was gone and only a smoky puddle of sticky, dark oil remained. Flames licked across its surface, growing ever larger and fiercer as the fire took hold.

The bars of the cage slid away when Malkus pressed the small button set into its outside wall. Everlyne threw herself at her brother and wrapped him in a warm embrace.

Together they stood at the end of the charred path the metal star had left when it had fallen from the sky. Together they watched it twist and melt and burn as the fire engulfed it.

Then, hand in hand, brother and sister turned and began their long walk home.

THE SCRUFFY PIPER

n the outer edge of the expanding human empire, Space Station Hamlyn stood guard against invasion. It was located in the Consodine Rift, through which any force would have to strike if it intended to attack the empire. In the early years of the Third Cyberwar, it was Space Station Hamlyn that stood between the frail humans and the advancing armies of the Cybermen.

The station was equipped with the latest X-ray laser weapons, and could withstand almost any assault.

The Cybermen, for their part, were well aware that Hamlyn's X-ray lasers would penetrate the hulls of even their most advanced battleships, so they kept their distance, biding their time in a nearby asteroid belt. They knew that the only way they could launch a successful attack on Space Station Hamlyn was if the X-ray lasers were first put out of action – and, to do that, the Cybermen would have to somehow infiltrate the station.

Of all the weapons in their own impressive arsenal, the
Cybermen had one that was ideally suited to this task:
the Cybermats. Converted from small animals – just as the
Cybermen themselves were converted from human beings –
the Cybermats were small cybernetic creatures, each about
the size and shape of a large rat. They could be programmed
to complete a specific task, and could home in on human
brainwaves, targeting their victims and then destroying them.

The Cybermen hidden in the asteroid belt had access
to hundreds of Cybermats, all of which they flew to the
edge of the Consodine Rift. Too small to register on any
detectors, the Cybermats slipped past the space station's
weapons systems. They latched on to the outside hull of the
station, and burned their way inside. Then, the instant they
were inside the station, they resealed the hull behind them –
a momentary drop in air pressure was the only clue that
anything was amiss.

A single drop in pressure might ordinarily have been
dismissed as a false reading on the station's instruments, or
some sort of glitch in the atmosphere pumps. Dozens of
them so close together, however, soon attracted the attention
of the station's security chief. He ordered a search of the
sections near the outer hull where the pressure drops had
been recorded.

But the Cybermats were adept at hiding themselves;
their mission depended on stealth and concealment. They
intended to get to the weapons systems and destroy the
X-ray lasers before the humans even realised they were
there. If they were detected, the Cybermats could fight
their way through but, like their masters, they preferred to

keep to the shadows and strike in secret.

So, when the security chief's guards searched the outer hull, they did not find a single Cybermat. What they did find, however, was a large blue box that had mysteriously appeared in one of the loading bays.

As the guards stared in surprise, wondering what exactly the box was and just how it had got there, a door at the front swung open. A scruffy man in a dark, baggy jacket and checked trousers stepped out. He wore an interested expression that soon turned to a frown of concern when he saw the guards approaching him with their weapons raised.

He turned and called back into the box, 'I think perhaps you two had better stay in here for now.' It was unclear who he could possibly be talking to, however, for it did not look as though there was much room for anyone else inside. Then he pulled the door shut behind him, and raised his hands in surrender. Two guards promptly stepped forward, took him by each arm and marched him to the chief, who was busy examining the station's security systems.

The chief was not quite sure what to make of this scruffy man. He appeared to be a complete fool, and yet somehow he had got past the most efficient security screening in the nine nebulae. What's more, he claimed to have no idea where he was but, as soon as the chief told him, he clapped his hands together and made comments that suggested he knew exactly where Space Station Hamlyn was located – and a good deal about its construction, much of which was confidential. His eyes gleamed when he caught sight of the station's main security systems.

'Tell us who you are,' the chief said to the scruffy man,

who had now made his way over the security systems panel.
'Where have you come from, and why are you here?'

'These drops in air pressure, do they occur often?' the
scruffy man asked, completely ignoring the question that the
chief had just put to him.

The chief was not used to being ignored, but he was as
baffled by the pressure drops as he was by the strange man, so
he decided he might as well answer. 'It's not something we've
noticed before today,' the chief admitted. 'But, as you can see
from the display, there have been dozens in a very short space
of time.'

The man nodded thoughtfully. 'I wonder . . .' he said.
'Do you mind?'

And, without waiting for an answer, the man adjusted
several of the controls on the panel, bringing up streams of
information. One of the read-outs he pulled up, the chief
noticed, required the chief's own personal password to access
it – a password which the man could not have known and had
not even entered. Whoever he was, this man obviously knew
what he was doing. In the chief's mind, that made him a
possible threat; for the moment, though, the chief let the man
examine the data.

'And your men were trying to discover what caused these
drops in pressure when they found me, were they?' the man
asked at last.

The chief nodded. 'I thought there might be some
problem with the outer hull, perhaps causing short leaks of
air from the station.'

The man nodded, smiling. 'But they didn't find anything,
did they? Apart from me, of course.'

The chief was forced to admit that they had not. 'They tested the hull, and it seems secure and intact,' he added defensively.

The scruffy man pressed his index finger into the corner of his mouth as he considered the situation. 'I've seen something like this before,' he said quietly. 'What about scratches?'

'Scratches?' asked the chief.

The scruffy man nodded. 'Scratches, yes – on the metal surfaces close to the hull. As if something hard, made of metal, had been dragged across it. Any sign of anything like that?'

The chief turned to the two guards who had brought in the scruffy man. 'Well?' he asked them.

The guards shook their heads. 'We weren't looking for scratches,' one of them said.

The scruffy man raised an eyebrow. 'Then I suggest you go and look now,' he said. The guards turned to the chief.

'You think this is important?' the chief demanded of the man, who blinked in surprise.

'Important?' the man replied. 'Well, I suppose that rather depends on whether or not you want your station to be left defenceless when the Cybermen attack.'

Now it was the chief's turn to look surprised. Only he and the most senior staff knew that, just an hour or so ago, Cyberships had been detected in the asteroid belt. Since they had the X-ray lasers to protect the station, there seemed no point in worrying the rest of the crew with the news.

'Go back through the whole area,' the chief told the guards now. 'And check for scratches.'

The scruffy man jumped to his feet and clapped his hands together. 'Splendid!' he announced. 'I'll come with you.'

The guards led the way to the access corridor that ran round the inside of the main hull – this was where the systems had recorded the drops in air pressure. The scruffy man fell to his knees and produced a magnifying glass from one of his pockets.

'Ah yes,' he said quietly, nodding. He straightened and stood up, then handed the magnifying glass to the chief and gestured for him to take a look. Sure enough, when the chief peered through the glass, he could see scratches quite clearly on the metal floor.

'And what does this tell us?' the chief asked.

'It tells us we're in trouble,' said the scruffy man.

One of the guards piped up. 'So what do we do, sir?'

It was the scruffy man who answered. He put away his magnifying glass, then dusted his hands together. 'We follow the scratches,' he said. 'Very, very carefully.' He dropped to his knees again and proceeded to crawl along the corridor, staring intently at the metal floor.

The chief and the two guards followed closely behind. After a few minutes, the chief began to wonder how long he should let this strange man crawl around the station before accepting that he was in fact quite mad and locking him up.

The man came abruptly to a stop. He turned to look up at the chief, indicating with his finger to his lips that everyone be quiet. Then he pointed to a maintenance duct in the wall just ahead of them. It was close to the floor, and the chief could see that the grille which covered the duct had been cut away. The man got to his feet, and stepped gingerly towards the broken grille, but the chief moved forward and put a hand on his shoulder to stop him. He gestured for the two guards to approach the duct first instead.

Closer to the duct now, the chief thought he could see something in the shadows behind the grille. There was a faint red glow. One of the guards bent down to peer inside the duct. As the chief watched, the red glow grew a little brighter, and resolved itself into two points of light. Points like eyes, staring out from the darkness.

Suddenly there was a blur of silver as something leaped from inside the duct and landed on the floor right in front of the guards. The chief stared in disbelief at the silver creature that had appeared, its eyes glowing red. Small antennae protruded from its head, and below the luminous eyes was a mouth filled with sharp metal teeth. A segmented silver tail swung slowly back and forth as if the creature was deciding what to do next.

'I think we should all back away very slowly,' the scruffy man said.

Before either of the guards could move, the metal creature's eyes glowed a brighter, more fiery red. One of the guards cried out in pain, clutching his hands to his head. His gun clattered to the floor. Moments later, the guard fell down beside his gun.

The second guard immediately raised his own weapon and opened fire. A laser blast caught the metal creature full on. One of its antennae was shorn off. Its tail convulsed, and the creature flipped on to its side. The guard stepped forward, taking aim again, but the scruffy man darted forward and caught his sleeve.

'Don't destroy it!' he said urgently. 'We need to examine
it.' He stepped closer to the metal creature, which continued
to spasm and twitch. 'I don't think it's dangerous any more.'
As he spoke, the creature gave a final shudder, and was still.

The chief was already calling for medical assistance for
the injured guard. The scruffy man quickly inspected the
guard and sighed. 'He needs immediate attention, but he
should be all right.'

'What is that thing?' the chief demanded as the man
carefully lifted the metal creature up and examined it.

'It's a Cybermat,' the man told him. 'One of the drops
in pressure you noticed was this little fellow cutting its way
through the hull and then sealing the hole up behind it.'

'One of the drops?' the chief said. 'But there were
dozens.'

The man nodded grimly. 'Which means the Cybermen
have sent dozens of Cybermats. I imagine they are
programmed to locate and destroy your defences. They're
operating in stealth mode at the moment, and only become
hostile if they are discovered. Unless we act quickly, they will
disable your X-ray lasers and then attack the crew – and the
Cybermen will follow.'

'So what can we do?' The chief's face was now set in
steely determination.

'We can examine this little creature and see what it tells
us.' The scruffy little man broke into a sudden smile. 'Now,
I wonder if you have a laboratory handy?'

In spite of the scruffy man's apparent knowledge and
enthusiasm, the chief still did not entirely trust him. He

stayed in the laboratory, along with the station's most senior scientist, as the man examined the damaged Cybermat.

'They home in on human brainwaves,' the man explained as he worked. 'Luckily, they can only latch on to one set of brainwaves at a time – although the Cybermen will overcome that particular limitation in a few decades.'

In light of the urgency of the situation they now found themselves in, the chief chose to overlook this last odd statement. He was starting to get used to the scruffy man's strange way of speaking.

'We need to find these Cybermats and destroy them,' said the chief. 'Guards, follow the scratch marks and let's hunt these pests down one by one.'

'You could do that,' the scruffy man said without looking up from his work probing the inside of the metal creature's head. 'However, I doubt you have time, or enough men – and you'll probably lose quite a few in the process. No,' he continued, looking up at last. 'My way is better.'

The chief looked stunned. He was not used to being told what to do. 'Your way?' he echoed. 'Are you telling me you know a better way to destroy these Cybermats?'

'Oh yes,' the man said, as if this was obvious. 'It's all a question of finding the right frequency.'

With the help of the station's scientists, the scruffy man set up a series of devices that could emit sounds on different frequencies. They then connected the devices to the inside of the Cybermat's head – a screen showed a magnified view of the creature's brain. The scruffy man watched the screen carefully while the scientists operated the devices. As the scientists tweaked the dials and changed settings, different tones sounded – some were low buzzes, others high-pitched wails that made the chief's ears ache.

'There!' the man exclaimed suddenly. 'That one again, please.'

By this time, they had been working for over an hour, with no apparent progress. Now, however, the man was hopping excitedly from one foot to the other. 'That's it!' he declared. 'That's what we need.'

The chief was thoroughly confused by now. 'You believe this sound alone will destroy the Cybermats?' he asked the man, who was furiously scribbling notes on a sheet of paper.

'Oh no,' the man said. Seeing the chief's disappointment, he smiled. 'But it will draw them to us. Unfortunately,' he went on, looking across the cluttered workbench, 'this equipment isn't really mobile.' He clicked his tongue as he considered. 'Play it again,' he ordered.

The note that played was neither high nor low, but a pleasant sound somewhere inbetween. The scruffy man frowned as he considered. 'About 440 hertz,' he murmured. 'Would you say that was D?' he asked. 'Or possibly C sharp?'

'I really don't know,' the chief admitted.

'Never mind,' the man said. He reached inside his jacket and pulled out a long tube with holes in it. He put it to his lips, covered some of the holes with his fingers and blew. The note that came out of the tube was exactly the same as the note the devices arranged on the workbench had emitted.

'Perfect!' the man said, lowering the tube. 'It's a recorder,' he explained. 'I'm quite good with it, even if I do say so myself.' He hesitated. 'Not sure my friends Jamie and Zoe would necessarily agree, but never mind. Now, let's

go back to that walkway round the hull and play hunt-the-
Cybermat.'

They returned to the part of the corridor where the first
Cybermat had been hiding. The scruffy man looked around,
nodded, then put his musical pipe to his lips and blew. A
single pure note rang out, loud and clear, through the station.

The chief was not really sure what the scruffy man
expected to happen – it all seemed quite mad to him. But as
he and the guards who had come with them watched, the
Cybermats started to appear. At first there were just vague
flashes of silver. Then, slowly, they all emerged from hiding.
The creatures slid out from ducts and shadows; they crawled
up from beneath the walkway and down the sides of walls.
Smiling as he continued to play, the man started along the
walkway and the Cybermats followed him. Drawn to the
sound of the scruffy man's musical note, more and more of
the metal creatures joined the line of silver that stretched
behind him.

Finally, when the strange procession had been all the
way round the outer hull, and the chief was sure there
could be no more of the creatures, the scruffy man led the
Cybermats to the secondary aft hold – this was where the
chief had decided the man should bring them. The area
had not been used for years, and the station wouldn't miss it.

Guards opened the main access hatch; it was rusty and
stiff with both age and lack of use. As soon as it was open,
the man marched inside, still playing his constant note.
The Cybermats swarmed after him like a great metal river.
They followed the man across the huge, empty space to the
far side of the hold. Then, the music changed.

The sound from the recorder warbled between several notes. The Cybermats swung around, disoriented and confused. As they turned back and forth, the scruffy man broke into a run and headed back towards the main hatch. Slowly the Cybermats began to realise what was happening, and turned to follow the man. He kept running, no longer playing the recorder. Behind him, the Cybermats seemed to sense where he was, and started back across the hold after him.

'Oh, my giddy aunt!' the man exclaimed breathlessly as he ran. 'Quickly – close the hatch as soon as I'm through.'

The chief hurried to help the guards to swing the cumbersome door back into place. Not a moment too soon, the scruffy man dived through the narrowing gap. The nearest Cybermat leaped after him just as the chief and the guards slammed the hatch shut; they heard the loud clang as the Cybermat collided with the other side of the heavy metal door.

The scruffy man stood wiping his forehead with a grubby handkerchief. 'They won't stay in there for long,' he told the chief. 'You'll have to move quickly.'

Already the guards were at work on the section's locking clamps. As soon as they were primed, the chief gave the order – the section was sealed off, and the clamps blown up. Without the clamps to secure it in place, the whole of the secondary aft hold detached from the main station. It drifted slowly away from Space Station Hamlyn, with the Cybermats still inside.

On the central screen in the station's control room, the chief and the scruffy man watched a close-up view of

the detached section as it drifted away. Already the
Cybermats were burrowing through the exterior. Gleams
of silver caught the starlight as the creatures began to tear
their way out.

As soon as the hold was far enough away from the
station, the chief gave another order. The main X-ray laser
swung round to aim at the detached section, then it fired.
The screen that the chief and the scruffy man were watching
disaplayed only static as the hold was blasted to pieces.

'That's the end of your Cybermats,' the scruffy man
said quietly. 'The Cybermen won't try that again.'

'Thank you,' the chief said. He turned to face the man.
'I think that leaves only one thing to be sorted out. You.'

The scruffy man looked startled. 'Me? But I don't need
sorting out.'

'I want to know who you are and how you came here,'
the chief said. 'How did you get past our defence shields?
Why are you here?'

The man sighed. 'I suppose I do owe you a few
explanations,' he agreed. 'The answers to all your questions
are in that large blue box you found me with.'

The chief's guards had been unable to open the blue
box. When the chief mentioned this to the man, he simply
smiled and said that he had a key – but he refused to hand it
over, explaining that it would only work for him. 'You have to
know exactly how to use it. My TARDIS – that is, the box –
has no ordinary lock, you know,' he told the chief.

So the chief and several of his guards led the man back
to the blue box. They watched as he unlocked the door.

'I promised you an answer,' he said, 'but I'm afraid it

may not be quite the answer you're looking for. In fact,' he admitted, 'it might only raise a few more questions in your mind.' Then, before the chief or any of the guards could follow him, he stepped inside the box and closed the door behind him.

'It's all right,' the chief told the guards. 'It's not as if he can go anywhere.'

But the chief's words were drowned out by the sudden scraping, trumpeting sound that echoed from the box. Then, slowly, as the chief and his guards watched in disbelief, the blue box faded away and disappeared.

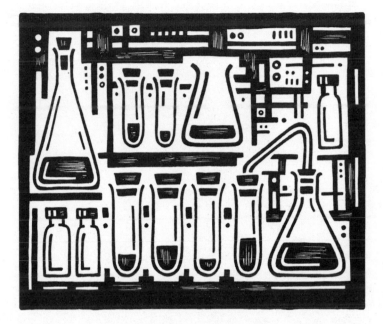

HELANA
AND THE BEAST

ong ago and far away, there once was a young woman called Helana who lived with her father on the edge of town. Helana's father was a scientist. When Helana was young, he had worked for a large corporation and was in charge of all their research and development, but when the corporation's profits fell the facility he worked in was closed.

From then on, Helana's father worked for himself, selling his expertise to whichever companies he could. When her father had work, things were good – Helana and her father ate well and could afford new clothes and trips to far off lands. Other times, though, when her father did not have work, Helana knew that things were tight. So, when she was able to, she worked in the town to earn a little extra money, helping in the library or one of the shops.

One day, Helana's father received a message. It was an offer of work: a private individual needed some research conducted and wanted Helana's father to do it.

'I shall be away for a few weeks,' he told his daughter. 'At least the money is good, and the work sounds interesting.'

Helana was not concerned. Her father often worked away from home, and she was quite used to coping on her own for a while. Gradually, though, the weeks became months, and Helana heard nothing from her father. She began to worry. She left messages on his communicator, but got no reply. She even went to the local constable to ask his advice, but he assured her that there was no need to be concerned – especially since money continued to appear in their household account each week. The constable was sure Helana's father was safe, and was probably just wrapped up in his work.

But Helana was not convinced, and she became increasingly worried until at last she decided to go through her father's messages to find the offer of work. When she had found it, she made a note of the address and programmed it into her transporter's navigation systems. Soon Helana had left the town altogether and was speeding through empty countryside in her transporter. It was a long journey, to a region she had never visited before. As the evening drew in, Helana still had not arrived at her destination.

Night fell, and Helana began to wonder if she would ever reach the address where her father was working. In the sky above her, a sliver of a moon was all but lost in the trees.

The transporter turned off the main road and headed down a narrow lane that ran through a dense wood. The lane ended at a pair of huge, elaborate metal gates set in a high stone wall. The transporter stopped. 'You have reached you destination,' the computerised navigation voice told Helana.

Cautiously, Helana got out of the transporter. As she approached the gates, she was able to discern a shadow in the distance that gradually morphed into the silhouette of a grand house. A long road wound its way towards the house, and a light burned in one of the windows.

There was no entry coder or communicator that Helana could see, so she pushed tentatively on one of the gates. It moved slightly. The metal was heavy and cold, and rust flaked off beneath her palms. She pushed harder, and the gate creaked and protested, but it swung far enough open to make a gap that she could squeeze through. Helana considered trying to open both gates fully, in order to bring the transporter through with her, but it had been so difficult to open one just a little that she decided against it – it would most likely take more strength than she possessed.

She was about halfway along the road to the house when a sudden flash of lightning illuminated the sky. Thunder split the silence. Helana hurried faster towards the house, hoping to get there before the rain started – but almost immediately a torrential downpour hit and, by the time Helana at last reached the front door, she was quite drenched.

Blinking the rainwater out of her eyes, she wiped her damp hand across her soaking face. She couldn't see a bell or a door knocker, so she hammered on the door with her fist, as hard and as loud as she could. She heard nothing except the distant rumble of thunder and the splashing of the rain. Just as she was about to knock again, she noticed the sound of heavy footsteps nearing the door, then heard several bolts being drawn back and a key turning in the lock.

The door swung open.

At first, Helana could only make out the vague, dark outline of an enormous figure standing in the doorway. But, when a new flash of lightning split the sky, Helana saw the face staring down at her. And she screamed.

The creature that stood in the doorway was something between a man, a bear and a lion. His face was covered in thick, matted fur and a huge paw with long, sharp claws reached out to grab Helana's shoulder and drag her inside. The creature's breath was rancid and stale. With deep-set red eyes, he glared at Helana. Yet, even through her fear, Helana thought she detected a flicker of kindness buried somewhere deep in those eyes.

'Who are you?' the beast growled. 'What do you want here?'

Helana was too terrified to speak. Taking a deep breath, she tried to remind herself that the creature had not hurt her – it had merely pulled her in out of the rain – and that the questions it was asking were not unreasonable.

'My name is Helana,' she stammered at last. 'I am looking for my father.'

'Your father?' the beast echoed. 'And what makes you think he might be here?'

'He came here,' Helana said. 'At least, I think he did. He is a scientist. He was offered work at this house.'

'Ah . . .' The beast nodded as if this made everything clear. 'Yes. You had better come through to the laboratory.'

Struggling to keep her fear hidden and under control, Helana followed the creature deeper into the huge house. The beast led her along corridors and down flights of stone steps until they arrived at a heavy wooden door studded with iron rivets. The beast turned a huge key in the lock, drew back a bolt and pushed the door open. He stood back, gesturing for Helana to go inside.

With some trepidation, she entered the room, half afraid that the door would slam shut behind her and that she would hear the key turn and the bolt being shot across to lock her inside. But the huge, hairy creature followed her into the cavernous, dimly lit chamber beyond the door.

At once Helana's fears were forgotten, swept away by a wave of relief when she saw the figure on the far side of the room staring at her in disbelief. Helana ignored the heavy wooden workbench, glassware, monitors and electronics that filled the room. She ran past it all without even noticing. Her attention was fixed on the man now facing her. Her father.

She ran into his arms, and they held each other close for a long time. Only as they stepped apart did Helana realise that the beast had gone, and the door was closed – closed, and locked. Her father nodded sadly at her. 'I am a prisoner here,' he told Helana. 'And now I fear you are too.'

The beast did not return for several hours. During that time, Helana's father told her how the creature had locked him away in the cellar laboratory and demanded that he work for him. 'But what he asks is impossible,' her father confessed. 'It requires a knowledge of genetics and DNA sequencing that I do not have – that no one in the world has.'

'Have you told him that?' Helana asked.

Her father shook his head and looked away. 'I am afraid that if he discovers I cannot do what he asks he will kill me.'

They sat in silence for a while. 'I shall tell him,' Helana said at last. Then, before her father could protest, she went on.

'Sooner or later he will realise that your work is going nowhere, and what will the consequences be then? No. We must tell him now – better to tell him the truth sooner than let his anger grow worse with time.'

Her father sighed. 'You may be right,' he conceded. 'Despite his temper and all the threats he makes, I do believe there is some decency hidden deep within him.'

'I think so too,' Helana said – and she remembered the touch of kindness she had glimpsed when she first looked into the beast's red eyes. 'You know,' she added, 'I think that above all he is sad.'

So, when the beast returned, Helana told him that her father's work was done.

'He has completed the task?' the beast asked, surprised. A burst of excitement flared in him, but it was quelled by Helana's next words.

'No,' she told him. 'What you ask is beyond him.'

'It's beyond anyone,' her father added quickly. 'I am sorry. My daughter felt you should be told the truth.'

For a moment, Helana and her father both held their breath, waiting to see how the beast would respond. The beast's massive body heaved, and they flinched . . . but all he did was give a melancholy sigh. He buried his hairy face in his great paws.

'So,' Helana said quietly, 'can we go?'

For a while, the creature did not answer. When it looked up, the fur round its eyes was damp from tears. 'No,' it said. 'If I must suffer without your help, then I must have company. I cannot endure this alone.'

'Please!' Helana's father sank to his knees in front of

the beast. 'I shall stay. I shall keep you company – but let my daughter go.'

'No!' Helana heard herself say, with such force that it surprised her. 'My father is growing old. He should not have to live out the rest of his days as a prisoner here. Let him return home. If you will promise not to lock me away and to let me live in the house properly, and if you will allow my father to visit once in a while, then I will stay with you. But let him go.'

The beast stared at her through his deep red eyes. 'You would stay in order that your father might go free?'

'Yes,' Helana said. 'I would.'

'But aren't you afraid of me?' the beast asked.

'When I first saw you, I was terrified,' Helana admitted. 'But now I sense that you are simply lonely, and I believe there is kindness in your heart. I believe you are just as afraid as we are, though of what I do not know. If you insist that one of us stay here with you then, please, let it be me.'

The beast stared at her. 'Very well,' he said quietly.

Helana's father was distraught. He tried to persuade his daughter to change her mind, but she was decided: her father's freedom was more important to her than her own.

The storm was over, and dawn was breaking. The beast allowed Helana to accompany her father back down the road to the transporter, which was still waiting by the gates. The creature walked a few paces behind, in case Helana should try to escape, but she had made a promise and had no intention of breaking it. When they reached the gates, she made no effort to follow her father through them.

'This is my home now,' she said, unable to keep the sadness out of her voice.

They hugged, and then Helana pushed her father gently away from her. She watched him climb into the transporter that had brought her here just a few hours ago, a few hours in which her life had changed completely. Then, once the transporter had departed on its long journey to the town, Helana turned and followed the beast back to the house.

The days that followed were empty and passed slowly for Helana. She sat with the beast for meals and in the evening. For the first few days, neither had very much to say to the other. Gradually, though, the coldness between them began to thaw. The beast and Helana began to talk to each other. Eventually, Helana even found herself starting to look forward to their evening meal, when they would sit on opposite sides of the large dining table and talk while they ate about things that did not really matter. Helana began to understand why the beast did not want to be alone in this huge house – here, just some company was a relief.

They talked about a great many things, but the beast never explained who he really was or why he looked as he did. If he had a name, he never told Helana what it was. Although he never spoke of it, and even though she had never asked, Helana was sure that he had suffered some secret tragedy. Sometimes, when there was a lull in their conversation, she would catch him watching her and in those moments his eyes emanated a sadness so profound Helana could almost feel it herself.

Helana had been in the house for an entire week before she found the library. The beast had learned that he could trust her not to try to leave, so he was happy for her to explore the house and its grounds. One day, Helana ventured along a corridor she had not seen before, and found herself standing at a large, heavy door. Despite its size, the door opened easily, and she stepped into a room so vast she could scarcely believe she had not found it sooner.

From the floor to the sweeping heights of the ceiling, the room was lined with shelves that were crammed with books. Helana walked slowly across the room, looking around in astonishment and delight. She loved reading and here, hidden away deep in the beast's house, was a library so huge it could keep her occupied and entertained for a lifetime.

At random, she pulled a book from one shelf and carried it to the large round polished-wood table in the centre of the room. In moments, she was completely absorbed in her reading, transported to a fantastical world. She lost track of how long she sat there . . . so she had no idea that she was being watched. When she finally looked up, though, she saw a strange man standing by a shelf, holding a book in one hand and watching her with ill-disguised curiosity.

'You shouldn't be here,' the man said. His accent was strange – slightly abrasive but somehow warm at the same time. 'Who are you? What are you doing?' he asked.

Helana stared back. 'I'm sorry. I'm just reading.'

'Well,' the man said. His heavy eyebrows knitted together in a frown, as if he was not quite sure what to say next. Then he nodded, still frowning. 'Good. That's good. Reading is good. You carry on. Don't mind me. Whoever you are.'

Helana found she was smiling back at him. 'I'm Helana,' she explained. 'I suppose I live here now.'

'What, with old hairy chops?' said the man.

Helana laughed. 'I think of him as the beast,' she said.

'Though he's not as beastly as he looks.'

'No,' the man said seriously. 'No, he really isn't.' Then he nodded thoughtfully. 'But I must be getting on. Things to do. Busy busy busy.'

'Aren't you going to tell me who you are?' Helana asked.

The man turned back, frowning. 'I'm . . .' He hesitated, looking around at all the books. 'I'm the librarian,' he said. 'Yes, that's it. The librarian. I work in libraries. Especially this one.' He turned to go, then turned back again. 'I don't suppose you know where the laboratory is, do you? I'm assuming there is one. Must be, in a place like this.'

Helana nodded. 'It's where my father worked. I'll show you.'

'Your father?' the man asked.

Helana closed the book she had been reading and replaced it on the shelf. 'I'll tell you about him on the way.'

Over the coming days, Helana spent much of her time in the library. She often saw the librarian consulting books and papers or on his way to and from the laboratory in the cellars. Helana came to understand how the books were organised; she found volumes she had not read since childhood, and discovered novels that were completely new to her.

She told the beast that she had found the library, and he seemed pleased that she had a way of occupying herself when she was not with him. One evening, in an unusually talkative mood, he told her that his father had collected most of the books, and that for a while he himself had continued to acquire novels and works of reference.

'Why did you stop?' Helana asked.

The beast did not answer, but turned away so she could not see his face.

'I'm sure the librarian would be happy to help you,' Helana said, hoping she had not offended him.

The beast lifted his face to her, his expression now one of bewilderment. 'What librarian?' he asked. 'There is no one in this house apart from you and me.'

He said it with such finality that Helana did not dare to argue – but, as soon as the meal was finished, she hurried to the library. There was no sign of the librarian, though she hunted through the maze of bookshelves and checked each and every alcove. He often spent time at one end of the library, where there was a strange blue cabinet that seemed out of place amongst all the books. But, when she looked, he was not there either.

Helana made her way to the cellars to check the laboratory. Sure enough, the librarian was standing by the main workbench. He held up a small glass bottle filled with a colourless liquid just as Helana entered.

'Who are you?' Helana demanded before the man could say a word. 'Why are you really here?'

'I'm the librarian,' he replied. 'I told you, remember?'

'But the beast says there is no librarian. He says there is no one in this house except for him and me,' she retorted.

The man's expression hardened. 'I'm here to help,' he said. 'Whatever else you care to believe, you must believe that.'

The man's expression was so intense that Helana found herself believing him. Before she could say anything more, the man held up the small bottle for her to see. 'My work here is almost done,' he said. 'This is why I came.'

'To take a bottle of liquid?' Helana asked.

'To *make* a bottle of liquid,' he corrected her. 'You have no idea how much research it involved. Your beast friend is lucky he has such a good library, and that I have an even better one.'

'But what is in the bottle?' Helana asked.

'His salvation,' the man told her. 'Yours too, I suspect. Here.' He handed her the bottle.

Helana stared at it, puzzled. 'What's it for?'

'It's for furry chops upstairs to drink, that's what,' the man said.

She hardly dared breathe as she asked, 'Will it kill him?'

The man's jaw dropped open. 'Kill him? What do you take me for! No. It will save him. Get him to drink it, and you'll see.'

Helana was still not sure, but she instinctively trusted the librarian. Not only was he knowledgeable, but if he had wanted to kill the beast with poison he would have been able to do so many times over by now.

It was not until the next evening that Helana got the chance to get the beast to drink the fluid. *Should I simply hand him the bottle?* she wondered. *Should I tell him about the librarian he did not know existed?* But she had no way of knowing how the beast would react. If the librarian was right and the liquid could somehow save him . . .

Towards the end of the meal, she took her chance to tip the contents of the small bottle into the beast's drink while he wasn't looking. Then, her heart thumping, she waited for him to drink. *Perhaps*, she thought, *nothing at all will happen.*

Something did happen, however. The beast downed his drink and almost immediately he began to choke and cough. His hands went to his throat and he stared accusingly across the table at Helana.

'What have you done to me?' he gasped.

She shook her head, trying to explain, but the words would not come. By now, the beast was on his feet, lurching round the table towards her and the only thing Helana could think to do was fetch the librarian. She ran from the dining hall, and could hear the beast staggering after her.

In the library, the librarian was sitting at the round table, his feet up on it and reading a book. He swung his feet to the ground and stood up as Helana rushed in, breathless and pale. She had hardly opened her mouth to explain what had happened when the doors burst open again and the beast fell into the room behind her.

At once the librarian was kneeling beside him, and he turned the beast over. The creature's eyes were closed.

'Oh, what have we done to him?' Helana gasped.

'Saved him, I hope,' the librarian said. 'A while ago, he was caught in an unstable time field. It's very rare, and very damaging. Evolution and regression all mixed up together. Resulting –' he gestured at the unconscious beast – 'in this.'

Helana had no idea what the man was talking about. 'What was that liquid?' she demanded. 'Was it poison?'

The librarian shook his head. 'It was a temporal antidote. It's what he was hoping your father could produce for him, but the knowledge and skill that's needed is way beyond anything on this backwards planet. No offence,' he added, glancing at Helana. 'I finally worked out the exact genetic code necessary to correct his DNA,' he went on, with just a hint of pride in his voice. 'Yes, look – it's working.'

Helana caught her breath as she saw what was happening to the beast. The hair on the creature's face seemed to be receding. His eyes cleared from red to blue. Where there had been a dark snout, a human nose appeared. The massive, hairy paws were suddenly hands – and one of them was reaching up towards Helana. She took hold of it.

'It's all right,' she said quietly. 'I'm here.'

'Helana,' the man who had been the beast breathed. His voice was gentle, not at all like the gruff tones Helana was used to. She still recognised the features of the beast in the handsome young man who slowly sat up and stared deep into her eyes. 'My darling Helana – I don't know how, but you have saved me.'

'It wasn't me,' she started to reply. As she spoke, she looked around for the librarian.

There was no sign of him.

They were alone in the library.

'I don't understand,' Helana said. 'Where has he gone?'

Her words were drowned out by the rasping, wheezing, scraping sound that came from the other side of the room. Over where the librarian's strange blue cabinet stood – or, rather, where it used to stand. The cabinet, like the librarian, had vanished into thin air.

ANDIBA AND THE FOUR SLITHEEN

nce, in a small town nestled in a remote valley far from any other towns or cities, there lived a young woman called Andiba. Her home town was unremarkable, except for its winery and distillery, which was known for producing the very best wine and vinegar anywhere in the region.

Andiba liked living in this little town. Several days a week she worked in a small bakery, selling bread and cakes to the local townspeople. The best part of her day was when Vash came in to buy bread. Vash, whose father was the manager of the winery and distillery, always seemed to be happy. His smile brightened Andiba's day.

When she was not working in the baker's shop, Andiba would go walking in the valley just beyond the town. She liked the fact that she was able to walk out into the countryside and, in just a few minutes, lose herself in the fields and woodland. She loved to walk alone, listening to the wind in the trees, the birds singing and the distant chuckle of the streams and waterfalls.

One day while she was out walking Andiba heard voices, which was unusual. Even though other people from the town did venture into the countryside, the valley was so large that Andiba rarely met anyone else – especially since she did not keep to the paths and roads, but explored the more remote areas. The voices were deep and strange, and this made Andiba wary. Being careful not to make any noise and to stay hidden in the trees, she crept closer to try to find out who the voices belonged to.

She found herself at the edge of a slope that led down into a shallow dip in the landscape. Below her was a large silver building. It was strange, sleek and curved, like nothing she had ever seen before. Standing outside it were four creatures – also like nothing she had ever seen before. They were tall with pot bellies and long arms that ended in clawed fingers. Their heads, which seemed to be balanced precariously on their necks, had round, almost childlike faces with big, dark eyes.

'The ship will be safe here,' one of the creatures told the others. 'No one from the town ventures this far afield.'

'Even if someone did find it,' another of the creatures said, 'they are such a primitive people that they would think it was just a building. The concept of space travel is far beyond them. And they cannot get in without the verbal entry code.'

This was certainly all beyond Andiba; she had absolutely no idea what the creatures were talking about. What was clear to her, though, was that they had come from far, far away, and she suspected that their intentions, whatever they might be, were not good. As the creatures' conversation continued, Andiba became sure of it.

'The orbital survey confirms that the best location to mine the madranite and other rare minerals is where the town is situated,' one of the creatures said.

'That is regrettable,' the first replied. 'But we Slitheen have never shied away from doing what we must to secure a profit. We shall have to destroy the town and everyone in it.'

Andiba put her hand over her mouth to stop herself gasping aloud. She had to find out exactly how these Slitheen planned to destroy her home town. She could not simply stand by and let that happen – but it was not going to be as easy as simply staying hidden and listening to their plans.

'We should continue this discussion inside the ship,' one of the Slitheen said. 'The main computer will have downloaded all available data on the town so we can start to plan our attack.'

The others nodded, and they all turned towards a door in the side of the metal building.

'Open, six one three,' one of them said. The door slid silently open. All four creatures made their way inside, and the door slid shut behind them.

Andiba frowned, wondering what to do. Should she hurry back to the town and raise the alarm? Who, if anyone, would believe her? And what could she usefully tell them? *No*, she decided, *it would be better to know more about the plans these Slitheen are making.*

Her heart thumping hard, Andiba made her way quietly down to the metal building. There was no obvious way to open the door – no handle or lever – so she repeated the words she had heard the Slitheen say.

'Open, six one three.'

Immediately the door slid open and, pausing for just a moment, Andiba stepped into the darkness beyond.

It took a little while for her eyes to adjust. When they did, she could see a corridor trailing off into the strange building. Further along the corridor, a pale green light spilled out of a doorway and Andiba could just make out the murmur of the creatures' voices.

As she crept cautiously towards the green-lit doorway, it became apparent that the voices were coming from yet further along the corridor. Andiba was curious to see what was through the glowing green doorway, though, so she peered carefully inside on her way past. Her eyes widened in surprise and disbelief.

Beyond the doorway lay a room bathed in the green glow; the light seemed to come from nowhere and everywhere at the same time. But it was what was inside the room that had startled Andiba. The room was full of crates and, because they did not have lids on them, Andiba could see that they were filled with jewels. There were diamonds, rubies, emeralds and many others she had no names for, all glittering in the pale light.

The voices from down the corridor had grown louder now, and Andiba had to remind herself why she was here. Tearing her eyes from the bounty in front of her, she stepped out of the room and carried on down the corridor.

Soon she saw light coming from another doorway further along. The Slitheen's voices grew steadily clearer and, as soon as Andiba could discern what they were saying, she stopped. She saw no point in going any closer to them than she had to.

'This distillery concerns me,' one of the Slitheen was saying. 'It produces wine, and also vinegar.'

There were muffled noises that sounded to Andiba like agreement.

'We must destroy the distillery before we can attack the town,' another of the creatures said.

'Obviously,' added a third. 'We cannot allow the inhabitants to have access to a weapon they could use against us – whether they know it's a weapon or not.'

A weapon? Andiba thought. *What could they mean?* Her curiosity outweighed her fear, and she crept a little closer.

'Then we must infiltrate this distillery,' the Slitheen who seemed to be in charge said.

'We only have one bodysuit,' another pointed out.

'One will be enough.'

Andiba had reached the doorway now, and she risked a quick look round its edge. She stared into the room for the briefest moment before stepping back out of sight – but she had seen enough. One of the Slitheen was holding up what looked like an empty human skin; the pale, dead features of the limp face were even more frightening than the Slitheen themselves.

Andiba backed away down the corridor. She had heard and seen enough, she decided. Now she had to get to the distillery and warn Vash's father that the Slitheen were coming. She hadn't been able to work out why but, for some reason, they were frightened of the distillery. And she had the distinct impression that it was not the wine but the vinegar that scared them.

The door to the ship had closed behind her. Andiba felt

a moment of panic. *What if the words that opened the door only worked from outside?* But, to her relief, the door opened at once when she said the words again.

Soon she was running up the incline and through the woodland back towards the town.

She was exhausted by the time she reached the distillery. The manager listened to her breathless story of strange creatures planning to destroy the town. As she spoke, Andiba's frustration grew; it became increasingly obvious that the manager did not believe a word of what she was telling him.

When she finished, the man smiled and told her it was an interesting story – she evidently had a very active imagination. Despite her protests, he showed her out of his office and pointed her towards the main doors of the distillery.

Furious and frustrated, Andiba made her way out of the distillery. She walked past the great metal chambers where the wine and vinegar bubbled away, fermenting. With every step, she became more determined to do something – the only problem was that she had no idea what she could do.

She was paying little attention to where she was going, and, on her way out the doors, Andiba collided with someone coming into the distillery. She stepped back, apologising. It was only when the person spoke that she realised who she had bumped into. It was Vash.

'Andiba?' he said in surprise. 'What are you doing here?'

Andiba was so relieved to see someone she knew that she almost burst into tears. Vash could see she was upset, so he led her to a bench outside and they sat down.

Andiba told him everything that had happened. To her

surprise, Vash did not laugh or tell her she was imagining it. His frown deepened as she went on.

'Do you believe me?' she demanded when she had finished.

He shrugged. 'Why would you lie? It doesn't sound like the sort of thing anyone would make up.'

Before either of them could say another word, a cart drew up close by. One of the distillery workmen hurried to help the rather portly driver down. In the back of the cart were four huge wooden barrels, just like the ones the distillery used to ship the wine and vinegar.

But it was the driver who held all of Andiba's attention. She had seen his wide, smiling face before – but limp and dead.

'That's him,' she hissed to Vash. 'The driver – it's one of the Slitheen.'

'Are you sure?'

'Of course,' she told him, shuddering. 'It's not a face I shall ever forget.'

The driver had gone inside the distillery. Vash hurried over to speak to the man who had helped the driver down from the cart. When he came back, he told Andiba, 'The man has gone to see my father. Apparently he has important business with him, about some new distilling process he has developed and which he thinks will interest him.'

'He's lying!' Andiba insisted.

Vash agreed. 'I think you're right, but Father won't listen to you. He probably won't listen to me either . . . but wait here while I'll go to the office and find out what's going on. Then we can decide what best to do.'

Andiba nodded. 'All right.'

She waited nervously for Vash, and every moment seemed to last forever.

After what felt like an eternity, the driver of the cart returned. He stood by and supervised several workmen while they unloaded the four enormous barrels and carried them inside the distillery. Andiba saw the workmen place the barrels in a corner of the main distilling area. Then the cart driver spoke to the manager again. Andiba could see Vash standing nearby, listening.

Andiba watched as the cart driver prised open one of the big barrels, then gestured to its contents while speaking to the manager and Vash. He then replaced the lid, and the three of them headed off into the main part of the distillery.

Andiba was beginning to wonder if the men would ever return when the cart driver reappeared. He walked briskly out of the main doors, barely glancing at Andiba before he clambered back up on to the cart and drove away.

Vash followed a few moments later. He sat down beside Andiba.

'I think you're right about the vinegar,' he said. 'Father gave that man a tour of the distillery, but he kept well back from the vinegar and wouldn't even pick up a bottle. It was as if he was afraid he would be burned by it.'

'What was in the barrels he delivered?' Andiba asked.

'He said it was wine. He promised us it is the very best wine we will ever taste, and he said he'd come back tomorrow to explain the process he used to make it. It's funny,' Vash went on, 'but he insisted we shouldn't taste the wine until he comes back.'

'Then I think we should certainly taste it now,' Andiba said.

Vash nodded. 'I agree. Let me talk to my father. Even he thought there was something odd about that man – I could tell.'

Vash's father was busy, but it was nearly the end of the working day. He agreed that after the workers had gone home and the distillery was shut down for the night he would examine the wine in the barrels the man had brought.

It was dark outside by the time Vash's father was ready. Most of the lights in the distillery were off, and the whole place had an eerie feel to it. Just as the cart driver had done earlier, Vash's father prised the lid off one of the barrels. He picked up a long ladle used for tasting the wine, and dipped it into the liquid. Andiba and Vash watched as he raised the ladle to his lips and took a sip. His expression did not change as he slowly lowered the ladle and tipped the remaining liquid on to the floor. It was colourless.

'Is it the best wine you've ever tasted?' Vash asked.

'It's water,' his father replied, then he turned to Andiba. 'You think this is somehow connected to the creatures you say you saw?'

Andiba nodded, relieved that he seemed at last to believe her story. 'They talked about infiltrating the distillery,' she said. 'And I think I know how they plan to do it.' She led Vash and his father away from the barrels. 'They said they only had one body suit, one human disguise, but I saw four of these Slitheen.'

'And there are four barrels,' Vash's father said thoughtfully.

'One is full of water,' Vash added. 'But what about the other three?'

'Perhaps we should find out?' his father suggested. 'But first we should make sure that we are armed, that we have some sort of weapon with which to protect ourselves if need be. Perhaps we should send for the constable.'

'No,' Andiba said. 'There's no time. Now that the distillery is closed for the night, the Slitheen – if they are indeed hidden in those barrels – could come out at any time. They plan to destroy the entire distillery.'

'It's fortunate then that we might have just the weapon we need right here,' said Vash.

'This is a distillery, not an arsenal,' his father pointed out. 'What weapon could we possibly have here?'

Vash smiled. 'Vinegar!'

It took some effort to persuade Vash's father that vinegar could be the weapon they needed; and Vash and Andiba were not entirely convinced themselves. But, based on what they had overheard and seen, it made sense. Why else would the Slitheen be so worried about the vinegar if not because it was a threat to them? First Andiba had overheard the four Slitheen talking about destroying the distillery, then the visiting cart driver had been afraid to go anywhere near the vinegar. Andiba, Vash and his father might not understand exactly what about the vinegar terrified the Slitheen, but it was increasingly clear that it might be their only – and best – defence against them.

Not far from where the Slitheens' barrels had been placed stood a huge vat of vinegar, waiting to be bottled. Vash and his father attached a hose to the outlet tap at the base of the vat, then Vash and Andiba held the heavy hose and aimed it at the nearest of the Slitheens' barrels. Vash had his hand on the

valve at the end of the hose; when he and Andiba were ready, Vash nodded to his father.

They watched anxiously as Vash's father pried the lid off a second barrel. Inside, the barrel was a mass of shadows; it was instantly obvious that there was no liquid in it. As the three of them looked on, the shadows began to move, as if they were uncoiling.

Suddenly a long, muscular arm lashed out, just missing Vash's father. He took a step backwards as the creature inside the barrel unfolded itself completely and stood up.

Vash opened the valve on the hose. Vinegar gushed out over the Slitheen.

For a moment, the Slitheen held its round, dark eyes on Vash and Andiba. For a moment, Andiba thought they had made a terrible mistake. But then the creature gave a roar of pain and anger, and exploded. Sticky, gooey fragments splattered across the floor.

At once the other two barrels began to shudder. Just as one shattered, sending wooden splinters flying across the room, Vash and Andiba turned the hose. The Slitheen that had been inside the now busted barrel hurled itself at the two of them – but the spray of vinegar from the hose caught it full on. Moments later, it too exploded into a glutinous mess.

The third Slitheen was just seconds behind. Having realised the fate of its fellows, it did not attack, but instead turned and ran for the main doors. Vash adjusted the valve on the hose, increasing the pressure of the liquid coming through. The spray lengthened, following the Slitheen until it eventually caught up and hosed down the creature's back. The Slitheen threw up its hands, and in an instant was gone in a squelching splat.

'Well,' said Vash's father, 'it looks like there'll be some tidying up to do in the morning.'

'What will the last Slitheen do when it finds out what has happened?' Andiba wondered.

'It will have to come back tomorrow to see if their plan worked,' Vash said.

'And,' his father told them, 'we shall be ready and waiting.'

The next day, when the cart pulled up and the large man climbed down, Vash's father hurried out to greet him. Vash and Andiba followed. If the Slitheen disguised as a man was surprised to see no sign of trouble at the distillery, he hid it well.

'We are so anxious to try your wine,' Vash's father said. 'Although we shall have to clear the barrels first,' he went on. 'We had some new equipment delivered after you had gone yesterday. We don't have much spare room, so we had to store it on top of your barrels. It's very heavy.'

The man nodded and smiled as though this made perfect sense. 'So long as we can move it to open my barrels,' he said. 'I think I can safely say that you are in for a surprise.'

'One of us is,' Andiba murmured to herself.

'Of course,' Vash's father said to the man. 'We'll open the barrels in a moment.'

'But first we brought some of our own wine for you to try,' Vash said.

Andiba handed the man a wine bottle and a glass. 'See how you like this vintage,' she said.

The man seemed reluctant to drink, but they insisted,

telling him they would open his barrels as soon as he had sampled the produce of the local vineyards.

So the man poured a small measure into his glass. 'It's an unusual colour,' he remarked as he inspected the wine through the glass.

'It's an unusual wine,' Vash said. 'It's traditional to drink it down in one gulp, and without smelling it. The joy in this wine comes from the taste alone, but it has a notoriously bad bouquet.'

The man did as Vash suggested.

At once his expression changed. His hand went to his throat. 'That's not wine,' he gasped.

'No,' said Andiba. 'It's vinegar.'

Moving quickly, she, Vash and Vash's father stepped away so that they were well back when the vinegar took its lethal effect.

'More mess to clear up,' Vash's father sighed.

Although she had enjoyed working in the bread shop, Andiba far preferred the job that Vash's father gave her, coordinating the business strategy at the distillery. She saw Vash every day, and every day they grew closer until one day they realised they had fallen in love.

Andiba knew that she and Vash would never lack for anything. She had not forgotten the strange metal building that was hidden just outside the town; she alone knew the secret words that would open the door. Inside, there were jewels and riches beyond imagination. Even after they had shared Andiba's precious discovery with the rest of the townsfolk, Andiba and Vash would be able to live more than comfortably for the rest of their days.

Vash's father could not have been more pleased, for his son was to marry a young woman whose bravery and intelligence were beyond measure. At Andiba and Vash's wedding, he served only the very finest of all his wines.

THE GRIEF
COLLECTOR

long time ago, when the universe was a much smaller and newer place, there lived a girl called Melina. Since before Melina could even remember, her best friend in the whole world had been a boy called Varan. As they grew up, the two remained the closest of friends and, gradually, their friendship turned into love. The day that Varan asked Melina to marry him was the happiest of her life.

But, if that day was her happiest, then the next was certainly one of the strangest. Melina's mind was already on the wedding; her thoughts were taken up with who to invite, what sort of dress she should wear and a dozen other tiny details. Every wedding-related thought caused her a flutter of excitement.

Melina's happiness was written across her face when she answered a knock at the door of the small abode she shared with several friends. Melina could not help smiling at the stranger who stood there looking back at her. He was a very

ordinary-looking man dressed in a dark suit and carrying
a briefcase.

'I hear that congratulations are in order,' the man said.
Then, before Melina was quite sure how, he was inside and
sitting on a threadbare chair with his briefcase balanced on
his knees.

'How did you know?' Melina asked, because she and
Varan had not yet told anyone about their engagement.

The man smiled thinly. 'You seem very happy,' he said,
and Melina had to agree.

The man looked coldly around the tiny, untidy room
before he went on. 'But how can you hope to remain happy
together,' he asked, 'when you are both so poor? I have seen
where Varan lives, and his place is just as small and rundown
as this. How are you paying for this accommodation? What
about your debts that remain to be paid? Do you even have
anything to eat?'

Melina felt her happiness begin to ebb away. Even if
what the man said was unkind, there was no mistaking the
truth of his words.

'But Varan and I have each other,' Marina told him.
'That's more than enough to keep us happy. Our love is worth
more than riches.'

The man nodded as if he had expected just such an
answer. 'I see,' he said quietly. 'Even so, wouldn't you rather be
free of such troubles? Wouldn't you like to live in a delightful
cottage of your own, with no cause to worry about how to pay
your way or where the next meal might come from?'

'Of course, but I don't see how that could be possible,'
Melina said.

The man smiled and opened his briefcase. 'Then it is lucky I'm here.' He took out some papers, and flicked through them, as if to remind himself of the contents, before saying, 'I have a proposition for you.'

Melina frowned. She was wary – she knew people who had borrowed money and been forced to pay back far more than they had been given. When she heard the amount of money the man mentioned, though, her eyes widened. Her mind immediately turned to all of the things she and Varan could do with it – a delightful cottage would barely dent such a sum.

'You are right to be wary,' the man said. 'But I promise you this is a good deal.'

'How much would we have to pay back?' Melina asked. 'And how soon?'

'Nothing,' the man said.

'Nothing?' Melina was uncertain. It seemed too good to be true.

'Not a penny.' The man handed her the papers. 'Think of it as a gift.'

Melina stared at the papers, but she was unable to focus on even a single word. 'But surely you must want something for it,' she said. She was having trouble believing that someone would just give away such a vast amount of money, and wanted to make sure she wasn't being tricked.

'All I ask in return,' said the man, 'is your tears.'

Melina opened her mouth in surprise. 'My tears?'

'Oh, not all of them,' the man said. 'Just the tears that you cry on one day: your wedding day.'

Melina laughed at that. 'But that will be the happiest

day of my life,' she told him.

The man smiled back at her. 'Then it will be a simple
debt to pay.' He stood up. 'Let me leave the document with
you. There are two copies. Read it carefully and, when you
are sure that you have understood it and everything is in
order, sign both copies. I shall return tomorrow to collect the
signed agreement and to give you the money.'

'What if I decide not to sign?' Melina asked.

'Then we shall both be disappointed. But I think you
will see that this is an excellent opportunity for you – for you
and for your future husband. Oh, just one thing,' the man
added, 'this must be our secret. Please tell no one of our
agreement, not even Varan. Tell him you saved up the
money, or inherited it, or that you won it somehow.'

The next day, the man returned, as he had promised he
would. Melina had read the document carefully, then read
it several more times. It was quite short and very clear: she
would be given the money and, in return, all that was asked
was that she surrender the tears she cried on her wedding day.
She could see no disadvantage at all, no possible catch.
And so she signed both copies of the agreement and handed
them back to the man.

He checked them thoroughly, then signed his own
name next to Melina's and handed one copy back to her.
'The money will be with you as soon as I leave,' he told her.
'Spend it wisely. On your wedding day I shall return to
collect your tears.'

'If I cry any,' Melina said.

The man did not answer. He simply smiled coolly,
then left.

True to her word, Melina did not tell even Varan how she had really come into so much money. All she told him was that she had won a lottery, and when Varan pressed her for details she simply said, 'Why does it matter, my love? All we need to worry about now is what to do with it.'

Varan, though still deeply curious about the money, couldn't help but agree. He promised not to ask any more questions, and together they searched for a home to live in after they were married.

They found the most wonderful cottage. It was on the edge of the town and close to the woods. Even after they had bought the cottage and all the furniture they needed, over half the money remained. Melina was sure that their life together in the cottage would be long and happy.

At last, the day that Melina and Varan were to be married arrived.

Melina made sure to be at the ceremony in good time. She looked beautiful in her stunning white robes. Her hair had been braided and her appearance was immaculate. The guests were waiting, and everything was perfect – except for one thing.

There was no sign of Varan.

The time of the wedding ceremony slipped by, and still Varan did not appear.

Varan's best friend tried to reassure Melina; he told her that he had seen Varan the previous night and all had been well. But, as time moved on and the guests became restless, Melina's anxiety grew. Varan's friend left to try to find him.

When Varan's friend returned, he was alone. His face

was grave. He could find no trace of Varan anywhere. It was as if Varan had vanished off the face of the world . . .

It became clear that there would be no wedding. Slowly, the guests drifted away. Eventually there was just Melina and a single guest left. She didn't know the man and assumed he must be a friend of Varan's. He was tall and slim, with a shock of dark hair and was dressed smartly in a deep blue pinstriped suit. He walked slowly up to Melina, and took her hands in his, looking deep into her eyes.

'I'm sorry,' he said gently. 'I'm so, so sorry.' Then he turned and walked quickly away, leaving Melina alone.

Finally Melina made her way back to the cottage. At this time, she and Varan had been meant to return there together, ready to start their married life full of joy and hope. Instead she was all alone, weighed down with despair and worry.

She sank into a chair, and buried her face in her hands. She had managed to hold back the tears until now – but, just as the first of them welled up in her eyes, there was a knock at the door. Melina jumped out of the chair and ran to answer it. She was sure that it must be Varan – or at least someone with news of what had happened to him.

Instead, waiting on the doorstep, she found the man who had given her the money.

'I have come to collect your debt,' he said, and pushed past Melina into the cottage. He opened his briefcase and took out a glass jar with an opening that was wide and curved, but Melina scarcely noticed what he was doing. The man set the jar on the table, and gestured for Melina to sit down close to it.

'Lean forward,' he said gently. He stood behind her and

took her shoulders, pushing her forward so that her head was above the jar. 'Let the tears flow.'

It was at this moment that Melina knew her dreams were ruined. There would be no happily-ever-after with Varan. She would never see him again. At last, she cried. The tears ran down her cheeks and dripped into the jar below. Her shoulders and her whole body heaved with grief.

When the jar was full, the man sealed it with a glass lid held in place by a metal clasp. Then he placed another jar on the table beneath Melina to catch the tears, which continued to flow.

How long Melina cried, how many jars she filled with her tears, she did not know. It was turning to evening by the time she realised that her eyes and her heart were empty. She had no more tears to cry. She leaned back and let out a long, shuddering sigh.

'Thank you,' the man said. He sealed the last of the jars and packed it into his briefcase. Then he opened the door, and was gone.

For a moment, Melina sat in silence. Her mind was numb. But slowly she realised that she was not alone. The man from the wedding – the man in the dark blue suit – was standing quietly just inside the door of the cottage, watching her.

'How do you suppose,' the man said quietly and thoughtfully, 'that he knew Varan would be missing?'

Melina shook her head. The question hadn't occurred to her.

'How did he know to come for your tears?'

Again, she shook her head. 'I don't know,' she confessed.

'Don't you want to find out?' The man raised his eyebrows. Then he smiled sadly, turned back towards the door and slipped away.

Whoever he was, the man was right. Melina did want to know more – in fact, she was desperate to discover what had happened to Varan. Without thinking, Melina hurried to the door. She grabbed a cloak and threw it over her wedding robes, then she set off after the man who had taken her tears. She hurried back towards the town as quickly as she could, and before long she saw him walking briskly in the distance. Keeping well back, making sure he did not see her, she followed the man through the outskirts of the town. It was getting dark by the time he reached his destination: a large mansion at the edge of town.

The mansion was set in its own grounds. From the road, Melina watched the man walk up a curving driveway to the house. He produced a key from his pocket, opened the door and went inside. Melina watched the house for a while, but night soon fell and it became completely dark. Finally, unable to see any more, she turned and started the long, lonely walk back to the cottage.

When she got home, she found the man from the wedding sitting in an armchair, waiting for her. 'I made tea,' he said, gesturing to a cup on the table beside another armchair.

'You keep turning up uninvited,' Melina said. 'Who are you? What do you want?'

The man was calm and spoke softly. 'I'm the Doctor,' he said. 'But, more to the point, who was the man who took your tears? Do you actually know anything about him?'

'He gave me money,' Melina confessed. She slumped down in the chair. Without really knowing why, she told the Doctor everything that had happened, finishing with her following the man to his house.

'So you don't even know his name?' the Doctor said quietly.

Melina shook her head and sipped at her tea. Then a thought occurred to her. She went over to her desk and hunted through the papers inside it until she found the agreement she had signed. There was no address on it, nothing to indicate who the man was – except for his signature, beside Melina's, on the last page. She realised that she had never bothered to try to read it. Now, she stared closely at the neat handwriting and saw that it was not a name at all. The agreement was signed 'The Grief Collector'.

'I've never heard of the Grief Collector,' Melina said. 'Have you?'

The Doctor nodded. 'Oh yes, I've heard of him. He's famous. Well, infamous. Well, notorious. Well, if you know who he is.'

'And who is he?'

The Doctor finished his tea and stood up. 'That's something else you should find out, I think.'

'Won't you tell me?'

'Oh that would be too easy. If you want to get your husband back – sorry, your fiancé,' he corrected himself, 'if you want to get him back, you'll need to visit the Grief Collector yourself.'

'But is it possible?' Melina asked, feeling hopeful for the first time since she had left the wedding.

'Anything's possible,' the Doctor said. 'Anything at all. Especially when it's driven by love.' Before Melina could respond, he added. 'I'll see you again soon, I expect.' Then, with a smile and nod, he was gone.

Now that she was alone again, Melina resolved to learn as much as she could about the Grief Collector. Over the next few weeks she began to ask if others had heard of him, and she came across his name more and more. She met people who had lost husbands, wives, children; people who had agreed to give their tears to the Grief Collector in return for money, or a piece of land, or a lucrative business deal . . .

The list went on. Every single person had thought that a few tears – tears they did not believe they would shed – were a small price to pay. Every single person had lost a loved one.

This cannot, Melina decided, *be a coincidence*. Somehow, the Grief Collector knew that people would disappear. How exactly, Melina could not guess – but she was determined to find out.

She gathered as many people who had entered into an agreement with the Grief Collector as she could, and together they went to the mansion at the edge of the town. Melina's plan had been for them all to confront the Grief Collector together – but the others wouldn't dare. They had lost so much already that they were afraid to risk anything or anyone else. Melina however, having come this far, refused to give up. Bravely, she walked up to the mansion alone. The others watched from the road outside.

But when she reached the door her resolve melted away. She glanced back at the others. Could she back out now, and beg someone else to go inside? As she hesitated, she saw a figure standing on the other side of the road. Leaning against a large blue box, which Melina had not seen before, was the man who called himself the Doctor. For a moment, despite the distance between them, her eyes connected with his. He nodded and smiled. And all Melina's uncertainty was gone in an instant.

Melina turned and knocked at the door, but there was no answer. She knocked again, louder, but still no one came. Melina turned back, checking that the Doctor was still watching her. Then she hammered on the door as loud as she could. When that still produced no result, she tried the handle. To her surprise, the door swung open – it was unlocked.

Glancing back at the people watching her from the street, and the Doctor watching from across the road, Melina took a deep breath then entered the mansion. She found herself in a large entrance hallway – at the end, a wide staircase swept to the upper floor, and ornate doors set with wooden carvings dotted either side.

Melina stood still for a moment while she decided what to do. She thought about calling out, but no one had come when she had knocked. Instead, she tried the door nearest to her. It opened into a very ordinary-looking drawing room. Disappointed, Melina tried the next door. This one led into a nondescript library, its walls lined with books. Just as Melina was about to close the door again and try the next one, she saw another door on the opposite side of the room.

Something made her sure that this was where she needed to go. Perhaps it was just a feeling, or perhaps it was to do with the fact that, whereas the other doors she had seen were intricately carved, this one was notably plain and ordinary. It stood out to Melina because it was so uninteresting. She crossed the library and opened it.

Beyond this door was another library of sorts. In this one, though, the floor-to-ceiling shelves were not filled with books. They were lined with glass jars.

Melina instantly recognised the distinctive shape of the jars. She knew at once what they contained. Every jar was labelled: a name neatly handwritten on card was attached to the shelf below each one. Melina looked around in horror. There must have been thousands of jars – *tens* of thousands – all filled with tears. The outpourings of so much grief . . .

Melina walked slowly through the large room, staring incredulously at the jars as she passed them. Somewhere here were the tears that she had cried for Varan. She could feel more tears welling up inside her, but Melina was determined not to cry. Not here.

At the back of the large room was yet another plain door. Could there be more jars, with more tears, beyond? Melina hardly dared to look – but she summoned what courage she could and opened the door . . . and stepped into a nightmare.

This room too was filled with glass jars. But these jars were far larger, and they were not filled with tears. These jars contained people.

Pale, haunted figures stood or sat inside their glass prisons; each jar held just one captive. Some turned to look at Melina. Some hammered on the inside of their jar, or shouted, but the glass was too thick for them to be heard. Some sat, silent and still, staring off into space.

Numb with disbelief, Melina walked slowly among the jars. When she peered between and through them she could see even more – they stretched into the distance, and everyone single one held a person trapped inside. Men, women, old and young – even children.

Suddenly Melina realised that she was staring at Varan.

He smiled sadly at her, placing his hand against the side of his jar. She placed her own hand on the other side of the glass from his – but all she could feel was the cold, unforgiving jar. This was too much for Melina. She screamed.

Every ounce of Melina's anguish and outrage was channelled into that one scream. A high-pitched shriek, it reverberated around the room. As she continued to scream, she fell to her knees.

At that same moment, the jar in front of her – the one that contained Varan – exploded into fragments.

Then, one by one, all around Melina, each of the jars shattered.

The people stepped out of their broken prisons, looking about them in astonishment and relief, but Melina scarcely noticed. Her attention was all on Varan. She grabbed him, and pulled him to her. Neither of them saw the other people making their way out of the room. Neither of them heard the words of thanks. They only saw and heard each other. As they stood there, holding each other tightly, they lost all track of time. Eventually, though, they drew apart, and Melina led Varan back through the room, now full of broken glass. The other prisoners had all made their escape.

The sound of a door opening made them stop and turn. Behind them, from the distant doorway on the other side of the room, a figure stood staring at them.

The Grief Collector.

'What have you done?' the man roared. His face was twisted into an angry snarl. 'I need my prisoners! You have ruined everything – you will both suffer for this!'

Furiously, he strode towards them, his feet crunching on the shards that littered the floor. Melina grabbed Varan's hand and they started to run towards the door through which Melina had entered the room. Behind them, they could hear the Grief Collector's cries of rage, and the glass crunching under his feet as he chased them.

'You cannot escape me,' the Grief Collector shouted, following them into the room full of tears. He flung the door shut behind him as he flew through it.

Perhaps Melina could have outrun the man, but Varan was weak and exhausted from his imprisonment. They had almost reached the door that would lead them out of the room of tears when the Grief Collector at last caught up with them. He shoved Varan aside, and grabbed Melina by the shoulder, spinning her to face him. All around the Grief Collector, Melina could see the light glinting on the jars of tears.

Varan was struggling to his feet, but Melina knew he was too frail to have any chance of fighting off the Grief Collector. So she did the only thing she could think of. She screamed again. This scream, though, wasn't out of fear or horror. It was deliberate, and full of anger.

The jars on the shelves behind the Grief Collector exploded. Clear, salty liquid poured down, splashing to the floor. The Grief Collector turned in alarm, and Melina

twisted out of his grip. She grabbed Varan's hand and
pulled him after her. As they ran, she screamed again –
and kept screaming.

Jars exploded all around the room. Shards of glass
rained down on the Grief Collector. His feet splashed in the
flood of tears as he ran after Melina and Varan. Yet more jars
shattered. The tears were now gushing down in a torrent.

The Grief Collector's feet slipped out from under him
and he fell.

Melina and Varan fled through the door, and Melina
slammed it shut behind them. Had they been able to look
back into the room, they would have seen the Grief Collector
struggling back to his feet. They would have seen the tears
crashing down on him and filling the room. They would have
seen him desperately trying to climb the shelves to escape the
rising tide of tears until, inevitably, it closed over his head.
Finally, the Grief Collector was engulfed by the tears he
had taken.

Melina and Varan saw none of this. Instead, they
hurried out of the library, along the hall and emerged
through the front door into the sunlight. There, they saw the
people who had come to the mansion with Melina waiting for
them, reunited with the loved ones they had lost. Like Melina
and Varan, they were crying – but the tears they were crying
were tears of joy, not grief.

As she held Varan tightly, Melina saw the Doctor over
Varan's shoulder. She saw him smile and nod, and pull open
a door in the blue box. She saw him go inside before tears of
joy blurred her vision. When she blinked them away, both the
Doctor and the box were gone.

THE THREE
BROTHERS GRUFF

here were once three brothers named Gruff who lived together on a farm far away from the nearest town. Although they were brothers, they were very different from one another.

The eldest, Carl Gruff, was incredibly strong. As well as being the oldest of the brothers he was also the tallest and broadest.

The middle brother was called Meklan Gruff. He was nowhere near as strong as his older brother, but he was extremely brave and was willing to take great risks to bring respect and glory to his name.

The youngest was Naze Gruff. He was of much slighter build than either of his older brothers. He was not very strong or terribly brave, but he was far and away the cleverest of the brothers Gruff.

The three brothers worked well together, each appreciating the talents of the others. Their farm was well run, and every few months the brothers would travel to the

town to buy provisions. While they were gone, the workers
they employed looked after the farm. The journey to the town
was long, but the brothers enjoyed having time together away
from the farm.

Part of the journey to the town wound through a
narrow valley with steep, rocky walls that made the whole
place seem desolate and grey. The valley was a stark contrast
to the rolling, open countryside of the rest of the journey.

One sunny afternoon, the brothers were travelling
through this valley on their way back home. They were in
high spirits, having found a provisioner who would arrange
for everything they had bought to be delivered to their farm
in the next few days. Free of the burden of carrying their
provisions home themselves, they walked through the grey
valley without any undue apprehension or caution, expecting
to emerge into the rolling countryside in a few hours.

But, halfway through the valley, Carl stopped. 'I don't
remember seeing that before,' he said, pointing to something
a short way up the side of the valley.

Meklan and Naze shielded their eyes from the sun,
which was low in the sky and shining along the pass. They
could just discern a large, spherical object that was almost
as grey as the rocks surrounding it. The way the sun glinted
on its textured surface suggested it was made of metal.

They approached the sphere curiously – but they
had gone only a few steps when they found their path was
blocked. It was as if there was an invisible wall in front
of them.

'But there's nothing there,' Meklan said, as he pushed
at the solid air.

Carl battered the invisible wall with his huge fists, but it didn't give even under his assault.

'We'll just have to go back and find a way round it,' Naze said, as practical as ever.

But they found they could not go back either – another invisible wall blocked the way they had just come. They felt all around themselves, and soon discovered that they were trapped inside a small area. While his brothers were testing the limits of the invisible cage they now found themselves in, Naze noticed a movement. He alerted Meklan and Carl and, as they stopped to look, a section of the metal sphere – which was just ahead of them – swung open like a door.

Out of the sphere stepped a figure. It began to walk towards them.

As it approached, it moved out of the bright sunlight and into shadow, and the three brothers Gruff could see it more clearly.

'A troll!' Carl declared.

It certainly looked like a troll. The figure wore dark armour of a type the brothers had never seen before, and carried its helmet under its arm. Small, deep-set eyes stared out from a head that seemed to be joined directly to the body. As it stared at the brothers, the creature licked a bloodless tongue over its thin lips and gave a rasping sigh of satisfaction.

'Who are you?' Meklan gasped.

The creature's voice was low and guttural. 'I am Commander Starn, of the Sontaran Assessment Survey. And you –' Starn paused to look at each of them in turn – 'you are nothing. You are material to be assessed, that is all.'

'Assessed?' Naze said. 'What do you mean by that?'

Starn continued as if Naze had not spoken. 'You will obey your instructions precisely and immediately, or you will be obliterated.' He pointed at Carl. 'You are evidently the strongest.'

'I am,' Carl agreed proudly.

'Good. Then you will be the subject of the first test.'

Starn lifted his hand, and the brothers saw that he had only two fingers and a thumb. He was holding a small metal device, and pressed a button set into its surface before reaching out with his other hand and pulling Carl towards him.

Meklan and Naze immediately tried to follow their brother, but they smashed into the invisible wall – Starn had apparently let it down just long enough to grab Carl, then instantly put it back in place. The two brothers could do nothing but watch as Carl was dragged out of sight by Starn; he might have been strong, but it was obvious that he was no match for the troll.

Naze and Meklan waited helplessly – but they did not have to wait long. Soon the troll was back, and this time it was Meklan that he dragged away.

Alone in the invisible cage, Naze set about thinking how he could help his brothers. One thing was certain: there was no way he could do anything while he was imprisoned. So it was that he felt a twinge of relief as well as fear when he saw Starn returning once more.

Naze allowed himself to be dragged across the valley. The troll's grip was incredibly strong; even if Naze had wanted to he could not have escaped. If he wanted to help

his brothers, he would have to bide his time and hope that
some opportunity arose.

On the other side of a rocky outcrop, they passed Carl.
The eldest brother was lying on his back on a flat rock.
Above and around him stood a metal framework and from
this hung a bar suspended by a chain. Carl had his arms
raised and was holding the bar. It did not look all that heavy,
but the muscles on Carl's arms were standing out and his
face was creased with the effort of holding it up. He could
not simply push it aside because the chain it hung from also
held the bar above him.

'A gravity bar,' Starn said, as he pushed Naze ahead
of him. 'I shall increase the weight of the bar until it
crushes him.'

'Why are you doing this?' Naze demanded. 'Why are
you torturing him?'

'It is not torture,' Starn growled. 'It is an assessment.
If we are to invade this primitive planet, then Sontaran High
Command must know if the population poses any risk to our
forces. This test assesses the physical strength of your species
and the force required to destroy you.'

Around the next outcrop, Naze saw Meklan sitting with
his back pressed against the steep side of the valley. A metal
disk was attached to his forehead. As the Sontaran pushed
past, Meklan stared at Naze; but Naze could tell his brother
did not see him. Meklan's eyes were glazed, and his face
contorted into a grimace of fear and horror. As Naze and
Starn moved on, Meklan suddenly screamed.

'What have you done to him?' Naze asked, trying to
turn back.

Starn shoved him forward. 'I have done nothing. It is his own imagination. I have merely reached into his mind and conjured up his very worst fears and nightmares.'

He nodded with satisfaction as another scream of terror reached them and echoed around the valley. 'Soon we shall know how brave he really is and, using that information, we can assess the psychological impact on your species of an invasion.'

Ahead of them, Naze could now see what he assumed was their destination. Standing on a patch of level ground was a metal structure with screens set into it. It did not look frightening but, having seen what was happening to his brothers, Naze was sure that he was in for the most unpleasant of experiences.

Starn pushed him roughly into the chair, and gestured to the screen. 'You will see a sequence of images,' he said. 'You will touch the image that does not conform with the others.'

'Why?' Naze asked.

'It is an intelligence test,' Starn told him. 'I am assessing the mental capacity of your species. We must know your weak points.'

'What if we don't have any weak points?' Naze asked.

'Every race has its weaknesses.'

'Even yours?'

Starn gave a short bark of a laugh. 'We Sontarans know how to turn our weaknesses into strengths.'

'How can you do that?' Naze asked – he was sure that if he could discover the creature's weaknesses it might be useful later.

'The probic vent on the back of my neck is especially vulnerable,' Starn said. 'But that weakness means I must always face my enemies, which is an advantage in battle. Now – begin.'

A series of symbols appeared on the screen. It was obvious to Naze which one did not fit with the others: all the symbols had rounded edges but one, which was angular and straight-edged.

Naze reached out and was about to touch the angular symbol when he hesitated. *Surely it would be better*, he thought, *if this troll creature thinks I am less clever than I really am.*

He touched one of the symbols with the rounded edges.

At once, Naze's whole body felt like it was on fire. He jolted upright in the seat and his teeth clenched together.

'An incorrect answer,' Starn said, as the pain slowly subsided. 'You will note that incorrect answers are rewarded with an electrical shock delivered through the chair. Continue.'

Despite the pain of the shocks, Naze knew that his best course of action was to appear stupid; that way he would seem to be no threat to the troll. So, as the puzzles appeared on the screen in front of him, he made sure to get most of the answers wrong; but a few he got right, because he figured that even someone who was truly stupid would answer correctly sometimes simply by chance.

Every time he deliberately chose a wrong answer, the pain shocked through him. It clouded his mind, making it difficult to think. Naze was worried that it would get so bad he might pass out – and that gave him an idea.

When the next electric shock jolted him upright in

the chair, he gave a great shudder, let out a loud gasp and slumped forward with his eyes closed. His head hit the desk in front of him and came to rest there.

Starn grabbed Naze by the hair and lifted his head. Naze kept his eyes tight shut.

'Weakling,' Starn snarled. He let go of Naze, and Naze let his head flop forward again, cracking it painfully on the desk.

Naze sat absolutely still for as long as he dared. He thought he heard the Sontaran moving away, but he could not be sure.

Finally, he risked opening his eyes. He sat up, trying to make it look as if he was just hazily regaining consciousness. He looked around, and was relieved to catch a glimpse of the troll-like Sontaran disappearing round the next outcrop of rock.

Naze got to his feet and, fighting back the pain in his head and the aches throughout his body, made his way after Starn.

It was an effort to ignore Meklan's screams of terror as he followed Starn through the valley, but Naze had to know where the Sontaran was going. They passed Carl, who still strained to keep the bar from crushing him, concentrating so hard that he didn't see his brother picking his way cautiously after Starn.

It was soon clear that Starn was making for the metal sphere he had first appeared from. As soon as Starn had disappeared inside it, Naze crept up to the open door. He could hear voices from inside – were there more Sontarans? He risked a quick look round the door frame, and saw that

Starn was speaking to another Sontaran who looked exactly like him, but was simply a face on a screen.

Naze stepped back out of sight, listening carefully.

'Your report is late,' the Sontaran on the screen was saying.

'My apologies, sir,' Starn replied. 'It proved difficult to find the right material for experimentation, but I have now acquired three specimens and begun the programme.'

'Then hurry,' the other Sontaran ordered. 'If it we do not receive your assessment report in the next day, the Grand Strategic Council will conclude that the planet poses an unacceptable risk and will abort the invasion.'

'I understand, sir,' Starn said. 'I have some preliminary findings concerning the terrain and climate which I will transmit now. The data is detailed, so the transmission will take some time. After that I shall continue the assessment.'

Naze had no idea how long Starn would be busy transmitting his data but it sounded as if it would be a while. Naze knew he might not get another chance to help his brothers so, while their captor was occupied, he hurried away from the metal sphere and back along the valley.

Carl was still straining to keep the bar above him. This time he noticed Naze approaching and forced a smile.

'You were always the clever one,' he said. 'If any one of us could escape, I knew it would be you.'

Naze examined the metal structure that held the bar in place above his brother. He figured out how he could adjust it in order to be able to swing the bar aside and let Carl get out – but, before he could start work, a scream of terror split the air.

'I'll be all right for a little longer,' Carl said. 'Go and help Meklan first. It sounds like he needs you more urgently than I do.'

Naze was reluctant to leave Carl, but he had to admit his brother was right. Promising to come back as soon as he could, he ran towards the sound of his other brother's cries.

Meklan was still sitting with his back to the rocky valley wall. His hands were stretched out in front of him, as if he was fending off some invisible attacker. Naze grabbed his hands, but Meklan pulled them away.

'It's OK,' Naze said, trying to soothe his brother. 'There's nothing there. It's all in your mind.'

But Meklan didn't seem to hear him – he didn't even seem to know Naze was there.

Unsure of what else he could do, Naze reached out and prised the metal disk from his brother's forehead.

The instant the disc was removed, Meklan drew a long, gasping breath and slumped forward. A few moments later, he looked up and smiled weakly at his brother.

'What was happening to you?' Naze said quietly.

'I saw such terrible, frightening things,' Meklan said. He shuddered at the memory. 'Thank goodness they're gone now.' He struggled unsteadily to his feet. 'Where's Carl?'

Naze led Meklan back to where Carl still strained to hold the bar – but their brother was not alone. Starn was standing close by, watching carefully.

'That troll is so strong I doubt even both of us could fight him off,' Meklan whispered as they ducked out of sight.

'I think I might know a way,' Naze said. 'But we need to rescue Carl first.'

'Stay here,' Meklan said. 'As soon as you get a chance, help Carl.'

Then, before Naze could stop him, Meklan stood and walked towards the Sontaran. 'Commander Starn,' he shouted as he approached.

The Sontaran swung round and stared at Meklan. 'You!' he exclaimed. 'How did you escape?'

'Maybe you're not as clever as you think you are. Or, maybe *we're* cleverer than you think we are,' Meklan said.

Starn slowly approached Meklan, pulling a small metal tube from his belt. There was no doubt from the way he held it and aimed it at Meklan that it was a weapon. Suddenly the tube spat fire and Meklan dived to one side just as the ground where he had been standing exploded.

'I thought you were a brave warrior,' Meklan said, getting back to his feet. 'Instead you hide behind a gun.'

'I hide behind nothing!' Starn snarled. He pushed the metal tube back into his belt. 'I shall kill you with my bare hands if that is your preferred method of execution.' He strode purposefully towards Meklan, who backed slowly away.

Naze pressed himself into the shadows behind the rocks. As Meklan passed, he glanced at Naze and smiled thinly. A few moments later, Starn followed. His attention was fixed on Meklan, so he did not see as Naze edged out from where he was hiding and ran to Carl.

'Quickly,' Carl gasped as Naze reached him. 'I can't hold it up any longer.'

As fast as he could, Naze loosened the sections of the metal framework that were holding the bar. It seemed to take forever, with Carl grunting and straining all the time and the bar slowly slipping lower as his strength failed, but at last Naze was able to swing the top section of the structure aside. The gravity bar crashed down, narrowly missing Carl's head and clanging against the rock beneath him.

At once Carl was on his feet, breathing heavily and flexing his tired arms. 'We must help Meklan.'

'Wait,' Naze told him. 'I know how to stop the troll, but we need a weapon – something to hit him with.'

Carl grabbed a section of the fallen scaffold and wrenched a length of metal free. 'Will this do?'

Naze nodded. 'Perfect.'

Together they ran to Meklan. Starn had caught up with Meklan by this time and was holding him tight round the neck. His back was to the other two brothers as they approached, so he didn't see them coming. Meklan was struggling to break free, but to little avail; the troll's strength was more than he could resist.

Naze gestured at Carl to be ready to hit Starn with the metal bar, then he focused on the back of the Sontaran's neck. He had no idea what a probic vent could be, but the word 'vent' suggested an opening of some sort. Sure enough, Naze spotted a small hole right in the centre of the troll's thick armoured collar.

'There!' Naze yelled, pointing at the hole. 'Hit him there!'

Hearing the voices behind him, Starn grunted angrily and tried to turn, but Meklan held him back. Carl hammered the length of metal into the back of the Sontaran's neck with a resounding clang and Starn let out a strangled gasp. His legs gave way and he collapsed, releasing his grip on Meklan.

'Is he dead?' Meklan said, his voice hoarse from where the Sontaran had held his neck.

'I don't know,' Naze admitted. 'Let's see if we can carry him back to that sphere. He talks to other Sontarans there on a screen. They said that if he doesn't report the results of his assessment, they won't invade our planet.'

'Then we have to make sure he doesn't report,' Carl said. 'How do we do that?'

'We smash the screen,' Naze told him. 'And anything else we can find.'

The Sontaran was heavy and the three brothers were all weak from their exertions, but they managed to carry the troll-like creature back to the sphere. They dumped him on the floor inside. Starn groaned, but did not wake.

'Where's the screen?' Carl asked, hefting the heavy length of metal, which he still held.

Naze showed him. Carl swung the metal bar, and the screen exploded in a mass of fragments. Behind the glass, wires and cables sparked and fizzed. Carl swung the metal bar again, hitting out at the controls and read-outs. More sparks flew, and soon the interior of the sphere was filled with smoke.

'We'd better get out of here,' Meklan said, coughing.

Carl swung the metal bar one more time. Something exploded, and he jumped back. A noise filled the sphere, a steadily rising hum of power.

'I think that might have been something important,' Naze said. 'Come on!'

He led them quickly out of the sphere, smoke billowing after them. The humming noise grew louder and rose in pitch as they ran down the steep side of the valley.

When they reached the bottom of the valley, they at last looked back – and saw that the sphere was glowing a deep, fiery red.

Carl grabbed his brothers, one in each huge hand, and dragged them down to the ground. Moments later, the metal sphere exploded in a ball of flame.

'I don't think Starn will be making his report now,' Naze said.

Meklan chuckled. 'So no invasion after all.'

'Good,' Carl said. 'Let's go home.'

So, laughing and joking as if nothing at all had happened, the three brothers Gruff set off along the valley towards the open countryside and the path that led back to their farm.

SIRGWAIN
AND THE
GREEN KNIGHT

n a time many thousands of years past, a king named Halfur ruled the land of Barnakadon. He was an honourable and fair king. Every month, on the day the moon became new, he held a council of the greatest and bravest lords and knights of the realm and sought their advice and wisdom.

One day, when a council meeting had been in session for several hours, the king and his knights received an unexpected and unwelcome visitor. Lord Fodon had just risen to speak about the swine fever that was affecting many farms; he wanted to discuss what could be done to help the farmers. He had barely started when there was the sound of a commotion from outside the great hall where the council met.

The members of the council all turned towards the door, wondering what the noise could be. The heavy wooden door was kept bolted while the council was in meeting, but behind it they could hear shouts and cries, and the sound of breaking glass and objects falling.

Suddenly the bolt on the door sheared away from the wood and clattered to the floor. The door itself was ripped from its hinges. The wood splintered, and the door fell into the room.

A huge figure stood framed in the doorway. From his stance and bearing, it was obvious this man was a warrior – but the armour and the helmet he wore were unfamiliar to the king and his council. The warrior's armour was green and textured with scales like the shell of a reptile. His helmet covered his whole head, leaving only a thin-lipped mouth visible – a mouth as green and reptilian as the rest of the warrior's armour. His eyes were hidden behind dark glass.

King Halfur rose angrily to his feet. 'What is your business here?' he demanded of the warrior. 'None may enter without my permission while my council is in session.'

The warrior strode into the room. He stood centrally between the room's two long wooden tables and looked round at the assembled knights and lords. When he spoke, his voice was a rasping hiss like that of a huge snake.

'You rule here. I require your assistance,' the warrior said to the king.

King Halfur gave a short, humourless laugh. 'This is hardly the way to seek it.'

The warrior continued as though the king had not spoken. 'My –' he paused, searching for the right word – 'my temple is in need of repair. It has sustained damage.'

The warrior turned slowly as he spoke, his glassed-over gaze resting on each of the council members in turn. 'I need materials with which to make the repairs. I shall also require the help of skilled labourers – those who can work in metal, and men of learning and knowledge. You have these, do you not?'

King Halfur was stunned. 'I am the king,' he said, his voice booming angrily in the great hall. 'No one may make such demands. No one may disturb my council. The penalty for your actions,' he announced, 'is death.'

The warrior gave a rasping hiss that might have been a sound of amusement. 'You have rules and laws. I respect that. You are evidently a man of honour. I respect that also.'

'Yet you smash your way into my council and make demands of me,' Halfur said. 'I see precious little respect there. I see no evidence of honour in *your* actions.'

The warrior stood motionless for a moment before replying. 'In the interest of honour, I shall submit to your law,' he said.

'You would agree to your own execution?' one of the knights asked.

The warrior turned to face him. 'In order that honour is satisfied, I am willing to take a blow to any part of my body from any one of you assembled here.'

There was a murmur of surprise. 'Then you will die,' King Halfur told the warrior.

'Perhaps,' the warrior agreed. He lifted his hand and pointed at the king. The gauntlet he wore was more like a clamp than an armoured glove. 'If I survive, however, you must provide the assistance I require.'

Halfur met the warrior's masked stare. 'Very well.'

The king was sure this was a promise he would not have to keep. In moments, the warrior would be dead.

'Also,' the warrior added, 'whichever of your knights

makes the blow must surrender himself to me in exactly
one month and take a similar blow in return.'

'As you wish,' the king replied. 'Prepare yourself,
green warrior.'

There was little doubt as to who should make the blow
and execute the warrior. The bravest and strongest of the
king's knights was Sirgwain. A giant of a man, it was said
that his mighty sword could fell a tree. It was well known –
and had been proved many times in battle – that with a
single blow from his sword Sirgwain could shatter even the
toughest armour and kill the unfortunate knight wearing it.

At King Halfur's command, Sirgwain stood up and
walked slowly to face the warrior. Although he was one of
the tallest men on the council, Sirgwain barely reached the
warrior's shoulders.

He drew his sword from its scabbard, and the polished,
razor-sharp metal glinted in the sunlight that streamed
through the hall's high windows. Sirgwain gripped his sword
in both hands; it was so heavy that few people could even
lift it, but Sirgwain raised the weapon as if it weighed
almost nothing.

'Prepare to meet your doom,' Sirgwain told the warrior.
'This is the fate of all who oppose King Halfur.'

'Strike when you are ready,' the warrior hissed.

Sirgwain swung the sword in a wide arc above his head
and brought it crashing down on the warrior; it connected
with the upper part of the warrior's chest. King Halfur and
the other members of his council knew what would happen;
they knew that the sword would bite through the warrior's
breastplate and shatter his armour before smashing through

to his body inside. The warrior would then crash to the ground, and his blood would trickle on to the flagstones of the great hall.

Except that is not what happened.

Instead, when the sword hit the warrior's strange green armour, it glanced aside. Sirgwain struggled to keep his balance as his heavy sword unexpectedly changed direction. He stared in disbelief first at the sword and then at the warrior. The strange green armour was not even scratched.

For several moments, there was only a shocked silence.

Then the warrior spoke. 'You will arrange the men and materials that I ask for,' he said to King Halfur.

Halfur nodded. 'That was the agreement,' he said, his voice slightly strained as he struggled to stay composed and not show how disturbed he was. He indicated one of the men sitting close to him. 'Tell Lord Grantith here what you require, and he will arrange it.'

The warrior turned to Sirgwain, who was now returning his sword to its scabbard. 'I shall give this Lord Grantith directions to my temple,' he said. 'I expect you there in exactly one month from today, to honour the rest of our agreement.'

Sirgwain said nothing. He walked slowly back to his chair and sat down, his mind numb. It seemed unbelievable that his sword, which had never failed him before, had let him down. Sirgwain hardly even noticed as the warrior left with Lord Grantith.

King Halfur declared the meeting of the council over for the day. The lords and knights departed, but Sirgwain still sat in his place, staring across the great hall and seeing nothing except his sword glancing off the warrior's armour.

The next day, King Halfur summoned Sirgwain. The knight presented himself, and knelt in front of the king's throne until Halfur told him to stand.

'This warrior is like no knight we have ever seen before,' King Halfur said. 'I have provided the men and materials he asked for to repair his temple. He in turn has promised to return the workers unharmed when their task is complete. But, as you know, there was another element to our agreement.'

'Yes, Your Majesty,' Sirgwain said. His voice was strained.

The king leaned forward on his throne. 'No one will think any the less of you if you fail to meet the warrior at his temple at the appointed time,' he said quietly. 'This warrior is not from my kingdom, that much is obvious. Whoever he is, we owe him nothing. Honour has been more than satisfied by the provision of the workers and materials he asked for.'

Sirgwain drew his shoulders back, and stared back at the king unflinchingly. 'That may be true, Your Majesty,' he said, 'but *my* honour demands that I meet him as was agreed.'

'It was I who made the agreement, not you,' the king told him. 'You need not be bound by it.'

'I *am* bound by it,' Sirgwain replied. 'Just as I am bound to you. I shall present myself at the warrior's temple on the appointed day, as was agreed. If I am to die, then so be it. Honour will be satisfied, and Your Majesty's reputation will remain untarnished.'

King Halfur sighed. 'Very well, Sirgwain. I shall ask Lord Grantith to give you the directions to the warrior's temple.'

The king stood and stepped down from the dais where his throne was positioned. He put his hand on Sirgwain's shoulder. 'You are, and always have been, the bravest and most honourable of my knights. I wish you well, Sirgwain.'

Lord Grantith told Sirgwain that it would take several days to travel to the warrior's temple. It would take him to parts of the kingdom that he had never visited before, and some harboured their own dangers. Normally, Sirgwain would have relished the thought of facing and conquering such threats. But it was with trepidation that he set out this time, for he knew he was going to his death.

Much could be written of the adventures that Sirgwain had on his journey to the temple. He faced the Oberdark of Greer and survived. He encountered the Seers of Doom in their caves and emerged unscathed. He passed through the Valley of the Shadow without once hesitating or turning from his path. Finally, he entered the part of King Halfur's realm where the warrior's temple was located.

The night before he was due to present himself to the warrior, Sirgwain did not sleep. Instead, he lay on a soft, grassy bank beneath the cloudless sky and looked up at the stars. He felt empty and numb inside. Had his whole life been leading to this – to a final encounter with the green warrior at a remote temple? He knew that he had achieved much. He was the bravest, strongest and most trusted of King Halfur's knights. He had a place on the king's council. He had helped Halfur and his army defeat the forces of the Netherling Emperor and battled against the hideous Orcusts when they tried to invade from the south.

But, Sirgwain thought, as he stared up at the stars,

I have never fallen in love. I have never married or had children.
When he was gone, the other knights and the king would
drink to his memory and tell stories of his bravery, but there
would be no one to mourn him. He was, when all was said
and done, just another knight.

Slowly the stars faded and, as dawn approached, the
sky brightened. As the sun rose, Sirgwain got to his feet and
braced himself for what lay ahead. He still had several miles
to go, and set off through the countryside, enjoying the sun
on his face for what he was sure would be the last time.

He passed through a small area of woodland, and
emerged at the top of a shallow slope that led down into a
valley. In the distance, the sun glinted on something in the
same way that it glinted on the polished armour of an
approaching army.

Shielding his eyes from the sun, Sirgwain could make
out small figures moving about a large structure that looked
like it was made of metal – this was what the sunlight was
reflecting off. In front of a dark opening that must be the
main entrance stood another larger, distinctive green figure.

The metal building must be the warrior's temple, Sirgwain
realised. He had arrived.

He could feel the warrior's glass-covered gaze follow
him as he walked down into the valley. Despite the fear he
felt, Sirgwain did his best to maintain the bearing of a knight
of King Halfur; but he struggled to keep his emotions from
showing as he got closer to the strange temple. This walk
down to the temple seemed to Sirgwain to take longer than
all the rest of his journey had.

At last, he found himself standing before the green warrior.

'You have come,' the warrior hissed.

'That was the agreement,' Sirgwain replied, aware of the slight tremor in his voice.

'The work is complete,' the warrior told him. 'The men that your king provided have worked hard and well. I thank the king for his assistance.'

'I'm sure King Halfur will be pleased that they have performed their duties so diligently,' Sirgwain said.

'And so,' the warrior rasped, 'we come to the final part of our agreement.'

Sirgwain nodded, but said nothing. He did not trust his voice to remain steady.

The warrior reached out a huge hand towards him. 'I have no sword,' he said. 'Therefore I shall use the sword that you used to strike a blow at me.'

The warrior took the sword from Sirgwain and examined it. He held it up, allowing the sun to reflect off the sharp, polished blade. 'A good weapon,' the warrior said. 'One I shall be proud to wield.'

'Then get it over with,' Sirgwain said. 'I am ready.'

The warrior lowered the sword. 'Very well. But first, if you will allow me, a test.'

A short way from the temple there was a single tree. The warrior strode over to it. The tree was not large, but it had a thick, sturdy trunk. The warrior examined it for a moment, before inspecting the sword again. Then he stepped back and raised the sword above his head. As it sliced down, hammering into the tree, Sirgwain shuddered. In a few moments, that same sword – the sword that had served him so well for so many years – would slice down into his own body.

He knew that the armour he wore would offer no protection.
The way the tree cracked, bent and finally toppled, crashing
to the ground, was proof of that.

Satisfied, the warrior turned and walked back to where
Sirgwain was waiting. Their work done, the men who had
repaired the temple had gathered round the warrior and
Sirgwain. Among them, Sirgwain recognised metalworkers
and blacksmiths, carpenters and labourers, teachers and
academics. All of them watched, grim-faced.

Sirgwain bowed his head slightly, unsure where the blow
would fall. Perhaps the warrior would strike his head from
his shoulders, or he might slice the sword through his armour
and deep into his chest. Whatever happened, Sirgwain hoped
it would be quick.

'Look at me,' the warrior commanded. Sirgwain looked
up, staring back at the dark glass of the eye covers set into
the warrior's helmet.

'I did not think you would keep our appointment,'
the warrior said. 'Clearly you are a man of honour.
A worthy opponent.'

So saying, he raised the sword again and brought it
down on Sirgwain.

But it was not the mighty blow Sirgwain was expecting.
The sword cut through the air, slicing down to within a few
inches of Sirgwain's chest . . . then it stopped. The warrior
held it still for a moment before gently tapping the blade
against Sirgwain's breastplate.

'Now,' the warrior said, 'honour is satisfied.'

He lowered the sword and handed it back to Sirgwain.
'You were wise to keep our appointment,' the warrior said.

'Wise and brave and honourable. I salute you, Sirgwain, knight of King Halfur.' The warrior stepped back, thumping his right fist into his own left shoulder and bowing his head slightly.

Surprised and relieved, Sirgwain stammered his thanks and sheathed his sword.

'My temple is repaired,' the warrior said. 'These people have done their work. Please take them back to your king with my thanks.'

'I shall,' Sirgwain said. 'But what about you?'

'What of me?'

Sirgwain gestured to the temple. 'There is nothing here. Nothing but your strange temple. Do you live here alone?'

The warrior gave a rasping laugh. 'I do not live here at all,' he said. 'It is time for you to return to your king. It is time for me to leave.'

'You're not staying at the temple?' Sirgwain asked. 'Is it not your home?'

'All will become clear,' the warrior promised. 'My home is among the stars. Now go. Continue to live your life with honour and fight bravely with glory. Fear no one, and let everyone fear you. I bid you farewell.'

The warrior turned and walked into the temple. A metal door slid shut across the dark entranceway.

Sirgwain looked around at the people watching him expectantly. 'We had better make a start,' he said. 'We have a long journey to get home.'

The workers collected together their possessions and followed Sirgwain up the sloping hill to the small area of woodland which he had come through on his way here.

It was with very different thoughts that he set out on the journey home. He had arrived with fear and resignation; he left with optimism and hope. He had expected to die; now his whole life stretched ahead of him. He would live it with honour, as the green warrior had told him.

As they reached the edge of the woodland, Sirgwain paused. He turned and looked back down into the valley. The sunlight glinted on the metal walls of the temple, just as it had when he had arrived – but there was something else. Another light, shining out from the base of the temple.

As Sirgwain and the others watched, fire erupted from beneath the metal building.

Slowly, the whole temple began to rise into the air. It gathered speed, rising higher and higher. Sirgwain watched as the warrior's temple faded into the distance. Soon he could see only the tiniest point of light from the fire that propelled it into the sky. Just like one of the stars amongst which the warrior lived.